THE SHEIKH'S SECRET LOVE CHILD

DIANA FRASER

The Sheikh's Revenge by Seduction
by Diana Fraser

© 2021 Diana Fraser
ISBN 978-0-9951410-6-3 (epub)
ISBN 978-1-99-102102-1 (print)

A desert warrior, a beautiful surfer, a brief affair which puts them all in danger...

—Secrets of the Sheikhs—
The Sheikh's Revenge by Seduction
The Sheikh's Secret Love Child
The Sheikh's Marriage Trap

—The Sheikhs of Havilah—
The Sheikh's Secret Baby
Bought by the Sheikh
The Sheikh's Forbidden Lover
Surrender to the Sheikh
Taken for the Sheikh's Harem

—Desert Kings—
Wanted: A Wife for the Sheikh
The Sheikh's Bargain Bride
The Sheikh's Lost Lover
Awakened by the Sheikh
Claimed by the Sheikh
Wanted: A Baby by the Sheikh

For more information about this author, visit:
https://www.dianafraser.net

Zeeshan swept into the room, paused briefly to glance at his brothers—Rayan and Adam, who were seated in the informal lounge area—and continued on to the small, windowless boardroom which they only used for confidential meetings.

Adam gave a low whistle, and followed him through. "It must be serious if we're meeting here." He took a sip of his coffee and then placed it on the table, spilling a few drops on a computer screen. Zeeshan shot him a dark glare. Adam ignored it and grinned. "What the hell has happened, Zeeshan? Got woman problems?" He huffed a cynical laugh and took a seat. "Need my highly confidential advice?"

"He certainly doesn't want your advice. He needs to marry, not have mistresses scattered around the world like you," said Rayan, his hands on his hips, his brow lowered as he stared at his elder half-brother. "Haven't your advisers come up with any suitable matches yet?"

Zeeshan scowled at his two brothers' teasing. "There is more to life than relationships. Although neither of you seem aware of that anymore." He indicated the seat. "Sit down, Rayan. Something serious has come up."

Rayan raised his eyebrows in surprise but did as his older brother told him and took a seat. He didn't relax as Adam had. The three brothers were all very different, and no doubt it was the differences which made them get on so well.

"I called you both here for a reason. And I don't wish to be overheard." Zeeshan looked from one brother to the other, his serious expression instantly quieting them. "American intelligence has informed us that I'm still a target for the Russians." He now had both his brothers' undivided attention.

Even Adam sat forward, his normally casual stance immediately tense, his eyes alert. "We couldn't expect any other outcome after your interference with their arms deal."

"No. But I had no choice. If it had gone ahead, extremist factions would have been able to destabilize the region, funded by Russia."

"You prevented a civil war," said Rayan, "and you stopped our own country going to war as well. But, in the process, you've made yourself Russia's enemy number one. They won't either forgive, or forget, your actions easily."

"So it would seem. I'm told that Russia's Foreign Intelligence Service believes me to be the one thing which is preventing them from gaining a foothold of power in our region."

"But how can they do that?" asked Adam. "They would never be accepted by our people, or those of our neighboring countries."

Zeeshan looked at his youngest brother and shook his head. Adam had always been less politically savvy than either he or Rayan. Perhaps he shouldn't have protected him so much. He would need all his brothers' support and expertise in the conflict that was brewing.

"It won't be that obvious," Zeeshan said. "They'll be working behind the scenes, paving their way with money and favors which people will accept all too readily. The few people who are aware of the Russian influence won't care about it. Because they will have what they want—finance to give them power. They want control over our lands and they see me as blocking it. They're out for my blood. Only that will clear the way for them."

Zeeshan could see the shock on Adam and Rayan's faces. They both hid it well. He doubted anyone else would see through the strong, impassive faces they showed to the world.

"So what would you have us do?" asked Rayan.

"Be on your guard. I've been told that things are going to get messy. And we need to make sure that we all stay safe, that our loved ones stay safe, and most of all, our countries stay safe. The Americans and the British have come on side now. They know that this could be a weak point in their line of defense. So they are feeding us whatever intelligence is required. And I have every confidence that between them and us, we will be able to fight this threat. Now, let's get down to business."

Two hours later, with their plans for defense confirmed, Rayan jumped up and checked the time. "I have to get back."

Adam laughed. "Is your new wife controlling your every move?"

Rayan walked up to Adam and gave him a hard stare. "You have no idea the delights of having a demanding wife, but when you do it will be me who is laughing."

Adam scoffed. "When I have a wife she will do exactly as I tell her."

Rayan and Zeeshan exchanged amused glances, much to Adam's annoyance.

"You wait and see, it will happen as I say," said Adam. "Unlike you two, I can control my women."

Zeeshan's smile suddenly dropped. Rayan scoffed. "Whatever, brother. You keep believing your dreams if you like, but they are only dreams." Before Adam could respond, Rayan turned to Zeeshan. "Call me if there's any change. You kept this from us for too long. No more secrets, right?"

Adam laughed. "You're one to talk." He turned to Zeeshan. "But Rayan is right. This is too dangerous for any more secrets to come between the three of us. Tell us of any developments and we will be here, and we'll fight this together. And if you can make yourself scarce to keep yourself safe, so much the better. At least, until we can be sure there are no spies around."

"Where am I going to go to?" asked Zeeshan. "No, my place is here."

"Adam is right," said Rayan. "Until we can be sure that there are no spies in the palace, you won't be safe. You need to find somewhere to go even if it's only for a few days. It'll give security a chance to make sure the palace hasn't been infiltrated."

He knew they were correct but still he shook his head. "I'll be fine. We will *all* be fine. Go back to your beautiful wife, Rayan, and give your sweet baby a kiss from me."

"And give your beautiful wife a kiss from me," said Adam, before disappearing hurriedly out the door, laughing. Rayan scowled.

"He's winding you up," said Zeeshan.

"Maybe," growled Rayan, "but it works." He followed Adam to the door. "Call me for anything, Zeeshan. We mustn't let this get out of hand."

Zeeshan remained in the room, staring out the window at the two helicopters which rose into the hot, dry desert air. Dust swirled around the palace courtyard, before his two brothers went in two different directions. It felt good to have told his brothers about the increasing threat from Russia. He reflected on what Rayan had said. Secrets? He had secrets still which he didn't intend to tell either of them, at least not until he'd received a report from the private investigator he'd hired.

The secret he *hadn't* told his brothers did, indeed, endanger him, but it had nothing to do with national security, only the defenses of his own heart. And they'd been breached, devastated, destroyed. It was too late to protect those.

He glanced at the closed laptop and at the email he'd received as his brothers had entered the room. He hadn't had time to open it before. His finger hovered over the long-awaited message, but instead he closed his eyes and imagined the person who'd savaged the defenses of his heart. Tanned, lean limbs, long, curling golden blonde hair, streaming in the wind as she balanced on top of a surf board in the skimpiest bikini he'd ever seen. But he didn't smile at the memory.

Instead of opening the email, he opened the photo his PI had sent him in an earlier email, which clearly showed the woman he'd lost his heart to and who had vanished from his life as suddenly as she'd entered it. She looked nothing like his memory of her. She was standing on the beach, watching the surf championships from a distance. At first he'd been surprised, wondering why she wasn't surfing, wondering why she was clutching a voluminous light coat around her body in the wind. But then, as he'd listened to his PI's report, he understood, all too well. Other photos, taken when the wind had whipped the coat from her hands, showed she was clearly pregnant—around six months he'd estimated, based on his sister-in-law's Lauren's pregnancy.

Three months earlier, Samantha Cross had been here, with him. She'd spent three months with him. Three months of intense pleasure such as he'd never known before. Day and night, they hadn't parted, and they'd talked of the future. He'd even proposed marriage and had given her a ring. He'd imagined they would be together, forever. And then she'd gone, without a word, leaving his future stretching emptily before him. Never had he felt so alone. Never had he felt so betrayed, and that was saying something after what his parents had done to him.

He almost didn't want to know the answer to the question he'd posed the PI—find out the identity of the baby's father. Samantha's doctor had been happy to divulge privileged information for the sum of money offered. Greed—he hated it. It was at the root of everything bad in his world. But it also came in useful when he needed to buy information.

This time without hesitation, he clicked open the email from his PI and the attached doctor's report. He quickly scanned it before closing his eyes in an effort to prevent the slash of pain from entering his body. It didn't work. He jumped up and looked out the window, westward to where the surf championships had been in the United States.

Samantha was pregnant with *his* child.

His child. And she'd gone away—for whatever reason—and was on her own. He knew, first hand, how vulnerable a child could be without the support of devoted parents. And he wasn't about to let what he'd seen happen to his brothers happen to his own child.

Suddenly he knew exactly where he'd go to escape the threat of the Russians.

CHAPTER 2

*S*amantha ran up the foul-smelling stairs to the battered door and glanced down the stairwell, hoping she hadn't been followed, as she fumbled with the key. It wasn't exertion which made her gasp for breath as she tried to focus on pushing the bent key in the lock. It was fear.

Twice she glanced away at a sound, but it was only a cat suddenly pouncing on its prey—Samantha shuddered at the thought—or the sudden thud as a kid kicked a ball against the outside wall of the tenement block. And that was only the abrupt sounds. The run-down building simmered with noise 24/7—arguments, laughter and, late into the night, gunshots from the neighboring streets. But none of that was as bad as what she was running from.

At last the key engaged in the lock and Samantha stumbled into the small room. She fell back against the closed door, weak with relief. Willing herself to calm down, she pressed her hand against her pregnant stomach. Surely this kind of stress wouldn't be good for her unborn child? She heaved a big sigh and pushed herself away from the door, then automatically began to fill the kettle.

She shouldn't have gone to the surfing championships last week. She knew that, but she hadn't been able to resist it —they had only been a bus-ride away and, up until six months ago, her life had revolved around surfing. She'd followed the sport around the world, from New Zealand to Russia, until it had taken her to a place which had changed her life—Ahmar. And what had happened there meant she had to be constantly on her guard.

Cold water suddenly spilled over her hand and she turned the tap off, and switched on the kettle. She opened the box of teabags—she was down to her last half-dozen. She sighed, placing one in the chipped cup, and turned away from the sight of her poverty. Poverty was the least of her problems. What lay in store for her if they caught her would be far worse than stale bread and twice-used tea bags.

She just hoped that she hadn't been recognized at the beach. But then, why would she? She looked in the mirror. Gone was the fun-loving, carefree Samantha, replaced by a thinner face dominated by eyes that betrayed fear, like an animal being hunted. She was no longer tanned, but pale from spending her time hiding away indoors. She'd only ever been outside her room for necessities until the surf competition had lured her out. She'd taken a big risk leaving her neighborhood, but she'd felt increasingly trapped and had persuaded herself that one outing would be fine. She'd always been the life and soul of the party. If there was fun to be had, she'd probably set it up and made sure she'd enjoyed it to the full. So watching it from the side-lines went against the grain. She'd needed to see her old world, even if it had to be from a distance.

But how much longer could she do this? She'd already moved twice, concerned that people were following her. Just the hint of a Russian accent had her retreating into the shadows, ducking into shops, slipping out a rear entrance, running along alleyways and then leaving the shabby rooms which were all she could afford. And then moving on again, waiting in the dark for a Greyhound bus to take her to yet another destination.

She'd started out hiding in country towns—small places where she thought she wouldn't be found. But it took two near misses to make her realize that cities were the only places where she could be truly anonymous. Trouble was, they were also places which tempted her out of hiding.

Just like a week ago. She'd been foolish. She should have known photographers would have been there. They wouldn't have looked twice at her with her shapeless coat and trousers, but she'd been too close to the action and had noticed the photographer too late—just as he'd moved away.

Had he taken a photo of her? She didn't know and she couldn't take the risk of hanging around to find out, of having the photos seen on the internet by the wrong people. She'd lie low for the weekend and then move on. Just like she always did.

She looked once more at her reflection in the mirror, fingering the leather thread which held a sapphire engagement ring. It was the one thing she refused to take off. It meant too much to her. She only hoped it wouldn't prove her undoing.

BY THE TIME Sunday night had come around, Samantha was packed and ready for the overnight bus to take her to a new hiding place. She took one last look around the tiny room. She'd left no trace of the six weeks she'd spent hiding out here, surrounded on three sides and top and bottom, by packed humanity. She wouldn't miss it.

Suddenly there was a thump on the door. Samantha jumped and stepped away—three steps for each of three more thumps. They weren't knocks—a gripped fist had been used to strike the door.

"Miss Cross? Are you there?" Samantha released a sigh of relief at the sound of her landlady's voice.

She was becoming paranoid. She pressed her eye against the peephole and saw her landlady standing there, her dyed red hair a stark contrast to her pale, lined face. The woman's bright blue eyes were fixed on the peephole in an unsmiling intensity, which made Samantha frown. What did she want?

Samantha glanced at her bags and kicked them behind the broken-down couch. She'd paid her rent but she wanted to avoid any discussion about why she was leaving at such a strange hour.

Samantha placed her eye to the peephole again and waited. The landlady glanced to her left, and then stared back at the door and knocked once more. It was a different kind of knock this time, almost as if it hadn't been her who'd knocked initially. Samantha shook her head, trying to free it of the pervasive paranoia.

As it didn't seem like she was going to leave anytime soon, Samantha cautiously opened the door, wishing there was a security lock. The woman gave her a grim smile and shrugged before stepping away.

"What?" asked Samantha. Something wasn't right. Instinctively she took a step backwards and began to pull the door closed. But, before she could close it fully, a hand—a large, brown-skinned masculine hand—gripped the side of the door and yanked it open. She staggered away in surprise as the dark doorway, backlit by a lone flickering light, filled with the tall silhouette of a man whose face she didn't need to see to know.

"Zeeshan," she said, on an exhaled breath, gathering the loose folds of her coat around her stomach.

"You sound surprised," he said. "Were you expecting someone else?"

She was, but she wasn't about to tell him that. Despite the fact that it was a shock to see him, there was also a sense of relief that it wasn't the people she feared.

"I was expecting no one."

He pushed the door open wide, entered the room and looked around—taking in the leaking tap, the smell of damp and trash from the bins three floors down, festering in the heat of the alleyway. Her neighbors were arguing as usual.

"And this is what you left me for? To be on your own, in such a place? Seems a strange choice."

She followed him back inside and closed the door, not wanting the landlady to know any more about her than she'd already pieced together. A quick glance told her that her bags were close to hand in case she needed to grab them and run. There was no one else with him, for which she was thankful. No one to witness the scene, no one to coerce her into doing anything she didn't want to do.

Zeeshan stood with his back to her, looking out at the view, if it could be called that. A cracked window in the tenement block across the alley reflected the last of the sunlight into her room. His broad shoulders were outlined in amber and there was a stillness about him which was one of the first things which had struck her. He was contained, thoughtful, considered. Trouble was, as he slowly turned to face her, all that quiet intensity was now in his dark eyes, which were fixed on her. Shivers sank into her gut and lower. His penetrating gaze still had the ability to get to her, even though he looked upon her now with dark suspicion.

"What are you doing here, Samantha?" She noted that he didn't call her by the name he used to call her. No one else, but him, called her Sammie. It suggested an intimacy they no longer had. But she regretted its passing. There had always been something in the way he'd said her name—elongating the vowel like a sigh—which touched her.

She missed it. She missed him. But she'd never have him again and it was all her fault.

"That's none of your business."

"Is it not?" He took a step towards her, but she couldn't retreat—she had nowhere to go.

She shook her head, her mouth suddenly too dry to allow her to speak.

"I think it is."

The room suddenly darkened, as the sun slid behind a building.

She swallowed. "How did you know where to find me?"

"I had you followed, of course. How else?" He glanced down at her packed bags. "Looks like I got here just in time."

She swallowed. "In time for what?"

He took a few steps towards her until there was only the length of a stride between them—a distance which would have been unthinkable when they'd been together. Then, their bodies had been drawn to each other, like moths to a flame, from the beginning. In their short relationship, they hadn't been apart. Until she'd forced herself away.

"In time, Samantha, to take you home."

She shook her head. "Home? Your home?"

"Of course." He indicated the room around him. "Certainly not this. Even you, I doubt, could consider this to be your home."

"I'm not coming with you." Her nerves were betrayed by her voice, which sounded strained and higher than usual.

He sighed. "Yes, you are," he said, as if speaking to a recalcitrant child.

She shook her head. She couldn't go with him. If she did, he'd discover she was pregnant, claim her child, and reject her. It was only a matter of time before the truth emerged, and she knew he'd never forgive her. He'd send her away as soon as he found out about her. No, she couldn't go with him because she couldn't risk losing her baby.

"I can't come with you."

"You are wrong, but then you are wrong about so many things, aren't you? What I want, Samantha, and what *will* happen, is that you will come with me now, and we will board a private jet which will take us back to Ahmar."

She shook her head. It was impossible. She'd left him as soon as she'd discovered the extent of the trouble she was in. He wouldn't want anything to do with her after he'd discovered the truth. And yet here he was, providing a safe haven for her from the people who were baying for her blood—and more. Two evils, but which was the lesser of them?

"No, I can't. It's impossible."

He glanced at her packed bags. "It looks more than possible to me. It appears you have nowhere to go, nowhere else to run."

"You must forget about me."

She gasped as he took a step closer. "You mistake my motives. This is nothing to do with you, and everything to do with the baby you are expecting."

It was only then that she knew she'd been kidding herself. Of course he knew she was pregnant. No doubt he'd made sure he knew everything there was to know about her. She suddenly felt drained, as if all the fight had left her, and the lack of food and exhaustion took its toll. She swayed unsteadily.

His hand shot out and gripped her arm, and he lowered her into a nearby chair. "You are weak." His gaze narrowed. "This isn't like you, Samantha."

"How would you know?" she said sharply, angry with herself for revealing her weakness. "You were so busy pursuing your own pleasure, escaping the yoke of your own duties, that you imagined me to be someone I wasn't." It was true, but not in the way she knew he'd take it.

Not a muscle moved on his face. It was as if there were a screen between them, making him unknowable and unreachable. She didn't have a clue what he was thinking or feeling.

"We're wasting time. Come, my car is outside and my plane is waiting at the airport."

"You're not listening to me, Zeeshan. I'm not coming."

"You are. If you don't come with me, then I'll leave you here, and let whoever hired the photographer find you. The law, presumably. I don't know what you've done, and I don't want to know. All I know is that you will come with me now, or face the consequences here."

She felt the blood drain from her face. He'd guessed wrong about the law, but it would be worse for her if he'd guessed the truth.

"Ah, I see my information is correct. Good, that makes it easier." He picked up her bags. "Come. There's no time to waste. If I've found you, no doubt the police won't be far behind."

She pressed her fingers to her forehead, trying to stop the pounding. How had it come to this? Hunted by men, deprived of her liberty? Zeeshan was right. She *was* being hunted, but, it seemed, he still didn't know the full extent of it. She knew the Russian who hunted her wouldn't spare either her or her child. But Zeeshan would at least protect her child, even if she was cast out once he'd discovered the truth.

She pushed herself unsteadily to her feet. "All right, I'll come."

She realized then, for the first time, that he hadn't been so sure she'd come with him. It tweaked at her heart in a way she wished it wouldn't. She preferred him to be the domineering sheikh she'd first met. It helped her to keep her distance from him.

"Good." He opened the door and stepped back, ever the gentleman, unlike almost every other man she'd met. "After you."

They stepped outside into the dimly lit lobby and the door slammed shut behind them. For the first time since he'd arrived, she felt Zeeshan's arm around her. Somehow he sensed she needed support.

"Don't worry," he said. "I'm merely ensuring the mother of my child doesn't fall down the steps. You don't look as if you could manage half-a-dozen steps on your own, let alone three flights, where you're as likely to trip over a drug addict as a cat."

She didn't answer. Partly because he was correct, and partly because she was stunned at the connection she felt at his touch. Regardless of what she wanted, her body responded to him, just as it had the moment they'd first met. He was *her* man, and there was no getting away from that, no matter what she feared.

Outside the building, a limousine with darkened windows waited, its motor running quietly. Zeeshan helped Samantha into the backseat of the limousine which, by now, had a group of kids and curious adults admiring it, held at bay by four of his bodyguards.

Some of the onlookers called out as they watched Zeeshan help Samantha into the car. There was a growing sense of unrest among the crowd, of mutterings and shouts, which attracted others, and people began to push against the bodyguards. Within seconds Zeeshan's men were in the limo, and the doors slammed shut against a sudden barrage of tin cans. The driver muttered curse words which Samantha didn't understand as they drove off.

"Nice people you lived amongst," Zeeshan said sarcastically.

"Yes," she murmured. "They are."

ZEESHAN FROWNED and looked straight ahead. It was as if she were a different person. Gone was her vivacity and charm, and in its place was a fearful woman. Instinctively he knew there was more to things than met the eye.

At first, when she'd left, he'd been torn between thinking that she'd regretted her impulsive behavior of becoming his lover, and thinking that she was simply doing what came naturally—seducing a man and then moving on. Whichever it had been, it had been her choice. He'd been determined to track her down, to make sure she was safe, but had refused to follow her. But the baby had been the game changer. Just thinking that she hadn't intended to tell him she was pregnant with his child sent a surge of anger through his veins.

Luckily his phone went, focusing him on what he needed to do. But, as he talked, he couldn't rid himself of his acute sense of awareness that she was sitting beside him. As he listened to his minister update him on affairs of state, he sensed her tension, saw her hands were gripped into fists, was aware of one hand on her belly as if wanting to protect the child inside. It appeared that was the one thing on which they agreed.

He turned determinedly to look out the window as he continued his conversation with his minister. He made sure that the conversation didn't end until they drew up outside the airport. He wasn't usually a coward but he had no idea how to deal with this stranger by his side—a stranger who he felt compelled to touch, and to protect, but a stranger with whom he also felt extreme anger and frustration. She didn't want him. That much was clear. But, unfortunately, his body told him that he very much wanted her.

After they got out of the car he took her elbow and guided her behind his staff. They were ushered directly through Customs and the paperwork was swiftly completed. In silence, they continued along the corridors, with the smoggy LA sunshine—unreachable—outside the windows. As they waited for the staff to handle their bags, he noticed her look longingly out the window.

He stood beside her, following her gaze. "What are you looking at?"

"Something it seems I cannot have." She turned to him. "My freedom."

Without waiting for him she walked over to the staff, and he followed her. He didn't answer her. Not because she hadn't asked him a question, but because there was no point. Her freedom had been curtailed the moment she'd fallen pregnant. As had his.

He stopped and talked to the pilot as the steward showed Samantha around the private jet. He breathed a sigh of relief. He'd found her and she was his now, which was exactly as it had to be.

He glanced through the small cabin, beyond which lay his office and bedroom. He'd imagined she would go straight to the bedroom, but she sat on one of the lounge chairs while a steward made her comfortable. He sat opposite her. There was a part of him that wanted to confront her, force her to look at him and know what was about to happen.

He kept his gaze on her as she determinedly looked out the window. It wasn't until they were in the air that she dragged a resigned gaze to meet his.

"Are you happy now?" she asked dully.

He grunted. "Happy isn't the word I'd used to describe how I feel."

"Then what word would you?"

"Satisfied."

It was her turn to grunt. "Such a dull, undemonstrative word." She turned her gaze back to the rocky peaks and darkly treed valleys of the San Gabriel mountains, far below them.

"For a dull, undemonstrative man." He leaned forward. She was trying to get a rise out of him, he knew that. He should have expected it. In the few months they spent together she'd been constantly provoking him, teasing him, pushing him out of his comfort zone. And he'd loved it, then at least. Now, he didn't like it at all.

She shot him a direct look. "You're not dull or undemonstrative."

He held her gaze, his attention caught by the first words which were neither defensive nor goading. She bit her lip and looked away as if she'd been found out.

"I'm surprised you know what kind of man I am. You showed more interest in sex than anything else in our short time together." It was juvenile, of course, but it seemed she didn't bring out the best in him.

She swallowed. It shouldn't have been so arousing. She cast a wary glance around the cabin, but they were alone. Not that he'd have cared. At least the fear had vanished from her eyes now, replaced by something a lot more fiery. But still she said nothing.

He leaned forward, so she was forced to look at him. "I remember that night when you caught my gaze and you came directly over to me. It was clear what you wanted."

She grunted and pursed her lips. "That was before…" She trailed off inexplicably.

"Before what?"

"Before I knew who you were."

He narrowed his eyes in confusion. "And you wouldn't

have wanted me if you knew I was King of Ahmar? Being very wealthy and powerful is a turn-off for you?"

She glared at him. "Yes, if you must know. I'm not the kind of woman who only wants a man who is rich. No... It was..." She looked away but not quickly enough to hide the fact that she was holding something back from him.

"It was what?"

She shrugged. "Just that I didn't know your name, or your identity, when I first saw you. It was only later that I knew who you were."

He should have been flattered that she'd wanted him solely for himself, not for his status, but she was hiding something, something he couldn't figure out.

"Why would me being king put you off? It wouldn't most women."

She bit her lip uncertainly and avoided his eyes. "You won't believe me, but I need you to understand that I didn't know who you were when we first got together."

He frowned, unable to understand her response. A knock at the door startled them both.

"Five minutes," growled Zeeshan, and the door remained closed. "I don't know what the hell is going on, Samantha." She looked at him with startled eyes. "There are things you aren't telling me, but you will."

"How can you be so sure?"

"How? Because when I do this"—he reached over and touched her hand and her eyes widened—"you don't withdraw." Her hand trembled under his and he waited to see what she'd do. Her eyes darkened with a desire, which he too felt. No matter what either of them said, or believed, their bodies were meant for each other. "You will tell me what I want to know when you are in my arms, in my bed."

"That's not going to happen."

He huffed a wry laugh. "Of course it is. We couldn't keep our hands off each other while you were with me."

She swallowed, but didn't reply.

"You cannot deny it, Samantha."

"I don't," she murmured huskily.

"Good," he said. It took all his willpower to drag his hand from hers. "We agree on something anyway."

He reached over, and watched as her skin prickled with goosebumps. But he only grazed her skin as he pressed the button which would summon the steward. He sat back and steepled his fingers, looking at her. Her gaze was caught like a precious butterfly in his web. She couldn't seem to avert it.

"You must be hungry."

She shook her head.

"You must eat."

"I'm too tired."

"Then go to the bedroom to sleep."

Again she shook her head. "I'd rather sit here."

"Please yourself." There was another knock at the door. "It seems I'm wanted elsewhere."

He left her without a second glance. But, after he'd spoken with the steward, he returned, unable to settle. As soon as he opened the cabin door he saw something which caught at his heart. Stubborn to the end, Samantha was fast asleep. Still seated upright, she sat awkwardly.

He stood in front of her, unable to resist the temptation of watching her sleep. There was no flickering of the eyelids, nothing to indicate dreams or uneasiness, only the sleep of the exhausted. The overhead lights cast shadows which accentuated the dark smudges beneath her eyes, which he'd noticed earlier. But at least he couldn't see the fear in her eyes anymore.

She was different, Zeeshan thought. Something had happened to her and she'd changed. He had noticed it from the moment he had set eyes on her in that disgusting room in the Wholesale District. She was no longer the confident, golden, beautiful girl he had met in Ahmar. She was fearful, a shadow of herself. Something had happened between their last night together and now. And he hadn't a clue what, but he was determined to find out.

Samantha shivered slightly under the cabin's lowering temperature. He hated the fact that just the sight of her melted his heart. Hated the fact that he seemed to be conditioned to save everybody, including someone who didn't want to be saved, someone who, it appeared, wanted nothing to do with Sheikh Zeeshan ibn Mohammed Aziz, King of Ahmar—only his body. Unfortunately the two came together, because she was expecting his child.

He flicked a switch and her seat flattened into a more comfortable position. Then he reached up and plucked a blanket from the overhead locker and laid it over her gently, his hand lingering on her shoulder, as he tucked the soft blanket around her. She sighed and wriggled into a more comfortable position.

He stepped away quickly and flexed his hands, as he realized all he wanted to do was kiss her. *That* he would not do, not while she was asleep. But later, after she'd accepted him as part of her future, then anything went. Not least because he knew he'd then discover her secrets.

He'd been wrong when he thought her a changed person. The Samantha he'd known for such a brief time was still there, beneath that frozen exterior. And he knew that all he had to do was touch her to find the real woman.

He withdrew his hand. He couldn't go there, not yet. He returned to his study and shut the door between them. Trouble was, it wasn't all that lay between them. Secrets. They seemed to rule his life.

CHAPTER 3

A feeling of well-being filled Samantha as she dreamed she was a child, playing with her father under the mild New Zealand sunshine. She smiled to herself as she watched him run along the beach toward her, trying to fly a kite. Despite the keen wind, the bright red kite didn't gain any height and its long tail trailed behind his lean silhouette, skimming the dark, wet sand. He stopped in front of her and she absorbed every detail of his dear face. She couldn't believe it. Here he was before her, and the sadness from which she'd been running the past five years was lifted.

"Dad!" she said. "You're back!"

"Of course I am. I never left!" he said, giving her a hug. His warm embrace enveloped her like a blanket. She wriggled into his arms. She couldn't remember feeling so happy. His old sweater felt prickly against her cheek and she could smell his aftershave. Above all, she felt safe for the first time in years.

"I thought you'd died." Her words were indistinct as she murmured them against his chest. "I thought I'd lost you."

His laughter vibrated through her. She could feel it in her bones. "You haven't lost me. I'll always be with you."

She pulled away from his chest and looked up into his face, but she couldn't see the details she yearned for so much, the sun was too bright behind him. She lifted her hand to touch his face, but he laughed and stepped away before she could feel his familiar features under her fingers. He took another step backwards, the kite now forgotten, lying lifeless in the sand, and she suddenly realized he was leaving her. Terror gripped her.

"Dad, don't go!" She'd tried to scream, but the words stayed, unformed, in her throat. He stood only half-a-dozen steps away from her, but something more than that separated them now, because he was beginning to fade into the bright sunlight. She didn't think she could bear to parted from him again. "Please," she tried to say, stumbling towards him, her legs heavy and unresponsive, her arms flailing as she tried to push through the space between them. "Please..." she mouthed. "Please!" With supreme effort she shouted aloud and reached out into air which thickened around her, robbing her of the last vestiges of her father.

This time her voice rang out loud and clear, and the dream collapsed in on itself. She awoke to find herself wound up in a blanket—not her father's pullover—with the hum of the airplane vibrating through her body—not her father's laughter. She closed her eyes against the bright light which now filled the cabin—*not* the New Zealand sunshine of her childhood.

"We will be arriving soon."

Samantha turned with a start, scrambling to sit upright on the slippery leather seat, desperate to know what was going on—her mind still somewhere between her dreams and this nightmare of a world.

"The cabin lights have been turned on because we will be

landing in an hour." Zeeshan's voice was impeccably polite and impossibly distant.

She sat up and pushed her hair—made messy by her disturbed sleep—back off her face. Hard, dark eyes looked back at her—eyes that were so different to the ones in her dream, which had been full of love. "Of course."

She flung off the blanket, frowning as she tried to remember pulling it over her. She couldn't. It must have been one of the stewards. "I'll go and freshen up." She rose and looked around, realizing that she had no idea where to go. She must have been out for the count.

"Behind you, to the left."

She nodded and followed his directions. Only when she was inside the immaculate bathroom did she take a deep breath and lean back against the closed door. Shakily, she stepped forward to the mirror. What she saw there didn't reassure her. She looked confused and frightened. This wasn't her. She turned on the tap, splashing water over her face, and glared up at her reflection again. That was better. Then she noticed in the reflection that, behind her, a number of abayas hung inside a small wardrobe.

He'd thought of everything. But, for once, as she stripped off her clothes and turned on the shower, she was relieved. She didn't know where her suitcases were and, anyway, little of what they contained fitted her anymore. She didn't have that worry with the loose folds of an abaya.

Refreshed after her shower, Samantha dressed in the clean clothes which had been laid out for her. As she returned to the cabin, she had to admit that the abaya was far more comfortable than her own restrictive clothing. She glanced through the window at the coastline, which was drawing ever closer.

Zeeshan looked up at her with an initial wariness which transformed into a flash of admiration. It was mutual. It wasn't his white robes or tall build which gave him his presence, it was something innate, something she'd been instinctively drawn to the moment she'd first set eyes on him.

"Thank you for arranging a change of clothes." She glanced at the food which now covered the table between them. Her stomach immediately grumbled as she realized how hungry she was. "And the food."

She'd been intending to sit in one of the other seats but she was too hungry to stand on principle—this time, anyway. She sat opposite him.

"You're welcome. Although all I did was order it."

All he'd done was *think* of it, she thought to herself. But she wasn't in the mood to give him compliments.

"And the abayas?" He shrugged. "It will be easier for you to enter the country unnoticed that way." She was glad she hadn't given him the compliment.

She took a bite of a bread roll and piled some cheese, olives and fruit onto the plate.

"When was the last time you ate?" he asked.

"I don't know." She didn't care to elaborate, although she knew full well it that it had been a good twenty-four hours earlier, and then it had only been a hot dog. It had been cheap and irresistible.

"When was the last time you slept well?"

She glanced up at him, but Zeeshan wasn't giving anything away in his expression. All she could sense from him was a grim resolute determination that felt impenetrable.

"I don't know," she said, her words clipped neatly, betraying her irritation. She'd agreed to come with him—not that she'd had any choice—but she hadn't agreed that he could control her.

"It seems you don't know a lot of things."

"Correct." She shot him a dark look. "Including what it is you want from me."

"I think you know what I want," he said, his brow lowered, his eyes glinting darkly.

"I wouldn't have asked if I knew," she retorted archly.

"Then I have obviously given you credit for being more intelligent than you are."

Samantha bit back the flair of anger at his cutting remark. He'd never said anything like that in their short time together. But, she guessed, that was what happened when you walked out on a man who was used to getting his own way, accustomed to being in control.

"Well, it's obvious you don't want *me*, you've hardly said a civil word to me. So that either means you want me out of sheer pig headedness because I left you, or you want my child."

"*Our* child," he snapped back quickly. "*Our* child," he repeated.

Her mouth went dry. How could he know? "Why would you think it was *your* child? How could you possibly know?"

"There's the fact that the dates coincide with the first time we had sexual intercourse."

Sexual intercourse? Samantha flinched at the clinical expression which sounded tawdry, as if it were something he wished hadn't happened. She remembered it quite differently. Even if she'd been able to suppress her memories during the day, at night she'd re-lived their lovemaking in her dreams. She'd thought he shared the same opinion. Apparently not.

"And I know you haven't been with another man since you left me."

She sat bolt upright. "How do you—"

"And then there's the fact that your medical records show your child shares my DNA," he interrupted.

26

Samantha couldn't believe what she was hearing. She leaned forward, eyes blazing with indignation. "Are you telling me my doctor has revealed this information to you?"

He leaned toward her, meeting her anger with his own, one that she didn't feel equal to facing. She gritted her teeth in an attempt to hide her nerves.

"I'm not telling you anything of the sort," he said, his voice as cold as his eyes were hot. She wasn't surprised at his self-control. He'd displayed enough of that, to devastating effect in their brief affair together. "You can draw your own conclusions," he continued, "as to how I know, for a fact, that you are carrying my child."

She swallowed, forcing herself not to shift back in her seat, away from the power of his orbit which threatened to draw her closer. Her eyes dropped to his full, firm lips, remembering where he'd kissed her and the heat which had ensued. When she next looked up, his eyes, too, had dropped to her lips. She licked them and he lifted his gaze and held hers. It seemed they were both saying one thing and thinking another.

"You should have chosen a doctor with integrity, someone who doesn't have a price." His measured words were totally at odds with what she read in his eyes.

"I had no choice. I went with whoever I could afford. Even so I can't believe that he revealed so much to you. I should sue him."

Zeeshan raised an eyebrow and looked at her with disdain. "I am sure your doctor is fully aware that you are not in a position to sue him. Otherwise, he would have been less forthcoming, otherwise his price would have been far higher."

Samantha sucked in a harsh breath, and tore her gaze away from Zeeshan's dark flashing eyes, to look fixedly out the airplane window at the white-flecked sea, which was coming ever closer to them as they descended.

"I am the father of your baby," Zeeshan continued. "And I will *not* allow a child of mind to be raised by a single mother in poverty. Least of all away from me."

"You cannot keep me, or my child."

"Of course I can. Getting you to come with me was meant to have been the hard part. Instead you came easily. I wonder why?"

She had a feeling that the reason she'd come with him could easily be read by him. It could be summed up in two words—fear and exhaustion. The number of times she'd thought she was being followed and had left her lodgings in the middle of the night to grab a Greyhound bus to God knows where, to find a new place to hide. She'd known she couldn't keep running forever. And she'd also known, or had thought she had known, that of the two groups of people trying to track her down, Zeeshan was the lesser of the two evils. She closed her eyes and tried to focus on her breathing, trying to calm the sense of panic which filled her.

"I don't know the real reason why you came with me," Zeeshan said. "Or why you left me, or why someone else is trying to track you down. But I will find out."

She opened her eyes with a renewed sense of panic, but fixed them on the coastline which had suddenly appeared outside the window. The azure sea was fringed with white along the shoreline and, beyond the strip of white sand, was a wide stretch of green, topped with a jagged outline of palm trees. Beyond the green, shimmering into a mirage of heat, everything drained into the pale light of the desert.

Suddenly the plane banked and the city came into view, with its tumble of adobe-colored buildings studded with minarets and spires, all rising to a central plateau upon which a gleaming white building sat. The palace overlooked everything and, she now knew, controlled everything.

The seatbelt signs went on and the steward came to prepare the cabin for landing. Samantha adjusted her seat, clipped her seatbelt on and focused on the view through the window, relieved that Zeeshan was talking to the steward. During their affair, when he'd focused his whole attention on her, it was like nothing she'd experienced before. She'd felt like a plant nurtured in a hothouse, lavished with attention, touched with reverence. He made her feel like she was all that mattered, which was a giddying sensation, as well as a new one. But, now, when the attention was the opposite of adoration, she felt as if she could be burned by that same flame.

She only relaxed when he moved away to talk to the pilot. When he returned he took a seat at his desk on the other side of the plane. She closed her eyes as exhaustion stole over her once more, despite the long sleep. Is this what it was going to be like? A battle of wills and wits all the time? She sighed. She didn't know if she had the strength. She kept her eyes closed, feigning sleep, while they landed. She kept her head angled away from him and opened her eyes only slightly to watch the jet taxi across to the terminal. A phalanx of white-robed men stood in a row, waiting for the plane to come to a halt. A welcoming committee. But not for her.

It had been very different when she'd arrived in Ahmar six months earlier. Then, she'd entered anonymously, with only her backpack crammed into the overhead locker, enabling her to immediately walk out of the airport, hire a scooter and be on her way into the city. And there she'd stayed, in a small cottage on the sea shore, one bay away from where the surf beach was and a couple of miles from the city center. She'd come to join her Russian surfer friend, Kirill, who she'd dated for a short while. When Kirill had told her about the beaches at Ahmar she hadn't believed him. But as soon as she'd landed she'd thought it was the most beautiful place in the world. From the front porch of her rented room she'd seen the white palace glittering in the sun, its benign presence casting a late afternoon shadow across the city. She'd never thought, in a million years that she'd get to visit it. But, then, she'd never thought she'd have an affair with the king.

When she'd accepted Kirill's dare to attend a royal reception at a hotel and flirt with the tall, handsome man she'd seen a few days earlier, standing alone in an ante-room of the club where they'd been drinking, she'd accepted gladly. He was gorgeous, she was tipsy, and she'd welcomed a bit of fun. She hadn't known he was king and hadn't anticipated their chemistry and what it would lead to. And, most of all, she hadn't known the whole thing was set up with something far more sinister than fun in mind.

"Samantha!"

She turned to see Zeeshan standing by the door. She looked around for her bag, but it was nowhere to be seen. Someone had already taken it. Of course they had.

As she went to follow Zeeshan down the steps, her way was blocked by the co-pilot, who smiled politely but firmly at her. "If you don't mind waiting a few minutes, His Majesty will disembark first. The press is waiting for him."

She nodded. She guessed it wouldn't look good for the king to be seen returning from an overseas trip with a pregnant woman in tow.

When the coast was clear, she descended the steps along with a small group of men who gathered around her—no doubt under instructions—and they quickly made their way into a separate entrance. From there, an officer escorted her to a private passport control and through to a lounge.

"You will wait here, madam," said the man, taking his

place by the door, as if to make sure she didn't escape. Where they thought she might run to, she didn't know. Minutes passed while she paced the floor. Eventually, after speaking into a hidden microphone, the man nodded to her with a polite smile. "They are ready for you now, madam."

The heat hit her as the sliding doors opened and she walked out of the air-conditioned building. A sleek limousine pulled up to the kerb and the rear door opened. She hesitated, then ducked her head and looked inside. The man behind her ushered her forward, while glancing all around and listening into his earpiece. "Inside here, please."

She stepped into the darkened luxurious interior and found herself seated beside Zeeshan once more.

"I apologize for the cloak and dagger stuff," he said, after he'd checked his phone. "But it is necessary."

She gave a small grunt. She could imagine quite well why it might be necessary for the King of Ahmar to distance himself from a pregnant woman. It didn't take much of a leap of imagination to figure out that it wouldn't be good for his image.

"We will shortly arrive at the palace where things will be easier to control."

She frowned for a moment at the odd wording, then sighed and didn't bother to respond. There didn't seem to be much point. At that moment she felt like a leaf being tossed on a stream. All she knew was that she'd end up somewhere, and that somewhere had to be better than where she had been.

And it was, she thought as she and an official were dropped off at the rear of the palace, while the car continued around to the front of the building with Zeeshan.

She felt resentful at the implication she wasn't good enough to be seen with him, even while she understood it. But her thoughts were soon forgotten under the instant spell the palace and its grounds cast upon her. It had been exactly the same six months earlier.

Samantha was no expert in buildings, but she had always felt a strong affinity with water and, in this palace, apparently so had its architect. No doubt water was especially prized because of its location, on the edge of a desert. But, even for Samantha who was accustomed to living by the sea, the palace—with its abundance of water—had worked its spell on her.

The central courtyard of the palace was bustling with all the people and activity required to keep a palace running. From a magnificent central fountain, a network of narrow rills and waterways fanned out, creating a constant soothing splashing sound, a cooling of the hot air, and a beautiful pattern around which the day-to-day life of the palace carried on.

But she didn't have long to admire it, as they moved swiftly through to offices, and then up some back stairs, along another set of corridors, up another set of stairs, to a place she'd never been before. Samantha was beginning to wish the palace was smaller, because already there was no way she would be able to re-trace her steps, when they stopped abruptly in front of a large two-doored entrance way. It was decorated all around with beautiful mosaics and chiseled stone signifying that, whatever was inside, had obviously been important at one time. Her silent companion opened the door, looked around and then stepped aside for her.

She was surprised to find herself, not in a room, but on a long balcony which overlooked yet another courtyard with a central fountain. Except this one was empty of people and the fountain was much smaller and finer in design. She walked forward, placed her hands on the balustrade and looked down. There was a peace and serenity to the place which instantly soothed her. It felt like a sanctuary.

There was a firm click from behind her and she turned to see the door had been closed. The official who'd brought her was nowhere to be seen. She looked around. The open-air corridor on which she stood was decorated with ornate paintings and had doors at each end. She tried each door but they were locked. She glanced at the door through which she'd come and frowning, tried the handle. It, too, was locked. The official had locked her in.

She tried to suppress a growing feeling of panic, and went the only route which was accessible to her, down a sweep of marble steps to the scented garden below. From there, she looked up. Above her was an open dome along whose struts wound green climbers, providing shelter from the direct sun and casting a green hue across the courtyard. She walked directly over to the fountain and sat on its edge, dipping her hand in the clear, cool water. She couldn't help herself. Ever since she was a child she'd been drawn to water. Her father had teased her that she'd been a mermaid in a past life. She'd loved that idea as a child.

For a moment she had a flashback to the lodgings which she'd just left, comparing them to here. If she'd been able to describe the perfect place to live, it would be this. The sound of the sea wafted in on a gentle breeze through the open window. This rear quarter of the palace was furthest away from the city, closest to the sea. She could smell its reassuring saltiness on the air. She looked around at the doors which opened out from the central courtyard. If the rooms on the story above her were locked, the ones leading out from the courtyard were all wide open. She went through the first door and found an elegant sitting room. She went to the next and found a large library with smaller offices leading off it. The third was a dining room, more comfortable and relaxed than the rest of the palace.

On the other side of the courtyard she found the biggest and most glamorous bedroom she'd ever seen. The furnishings were rich, opulent and luxurious. Everything, from the four-poster bed with its red and gold drapes, to the gold leaf on the ceiling, to the exquisite rugs under foot, was designed for seduction. Even the chaise longue was big enough for two people. And then there were the mirrors. Upon all the walls, assorted shapes and sizes were hung, some with plain gold frames, others more heavily worked and decorated. She could see reflection after reflection of herself from different angles. It was unsettling and she looked away. She imagined how intense it would be if two people were in the room. She glanced at the bed and realized the mirrors were positioned with the bed in mind. This was a room for love-making. Of that she was sure. She just hoped that she wasn't expected to share it with Zeeshan.

Suddenly her phone pinged. Her heartbeat quickened as she reached into her bag and checked the sender of the message. She huffed out a deep sigh of relief when she saw it was Zeeshan. Even now, even here, where at least she was safe from the Russians who Kirill had introduced her to as his friends, the fear she'd been living with every moment of the past six months still surfaced. She wondered if it would ever leave her.

She had an hour before dinner. An hour by herself in which to figure out what the hell she was going to do in this world in which she'd found herself. How did Zeeshan see her? Was she a friend, a guest, or someone to be tolerated until she could give him what he wanted—his child? But she knew one thing. However he saw her, however he envisaged her fitting into his world, he was mistaken if he thought she could be locked up.

. . .

IT WAS late by the time Zeeshan unlocked the door to the wing in which Samantha had been taken. He looked around the dining room. The food was in the warming drawers to the side, as he'd requested, but there was no sign of Samantha.

He poured himself a glass of water and knocked it back. He'd had a stressful afternoon dealing with not only domestic issues, but the overseas threats which appeared to be escalating. He was not in the mood to be kept waiting by anyone, especially not by Samantha.

Suddenly the double doors opened and Samantha swept into the room, looking more like the woman he knew, apart from her rounded stomach. She was tall, elegant, robust and fierce.

"Why am I being kept your prisoner, Zeeshan?"

He sighed. He could have done without this. "You're not."

She put her hands on her hips, tilted to one side and gave a little huff which really shouldn't have been so sexy. He instantly forgot his annoyance.

"Then what do you call it," she said, walking to the door and trying to open it. He had the key in his pocket. "When all the doors are locked and I'm not given a key?"

"What do I call it?" He sat at the table and helped himself to dinner. He suddenly realized how hungry he was. "I call it keeping you safe," he said, not bothering to turn to address her. He continued to load food onto his plate. Suddenly he smelt her perfume, sensed her presence close to him. His skin prickled with awareness. How did she have this effect on him?

"Safe? From whom? I don't need to be safe. What I need, Zeeshan..." She placed a hand on his arm, forcing him to twist his head to look at her. His initial impression had been correct. She looked wonderful. She'd recovered from the flight, and she looked well rested and strong again, even though she'd lost weight around her face. "What I need," she repeated, "is to be free."

He shrugged and continued to spoon too much food onto his plate. He wasn't *that* hungry but he wanted to keep his hands occupied, otherwise he was in danger of turning to her, putting his arms around her and bringing her hard against him. "Unfortunately, at the moment, that is one thing you cannot be."

"Why not?" She gripped his arm.

"Because"—he turned to her with a controlled weariness—"for some reason, which neither me, nor my advisers, can fathom, someone is after you, and I don't intend my child to be taken away from me. Is that reason enough?"

She glared at him, and her lips tightened as he knew that there was little she could say to contradict him. Not without telling him the truth, and he didn't fool himself that she was going to do that—yet. She grunted with frustration, withdrew her hand and walked over to the window, throwing it open to the sea air, inhaling deeply.

He understood her instinct. He was exactly the same.

"So how come you just happen to have a ready-made, secure suite of rooms available for me?"

"I don't. These rooms were already secure." He shot her a long, hard look, waiting for the inevitable question.

She narrowed her eyes in confusion. "How come? Do you make a habit of going around the world, bringing defenseless women back here on a whim?"

"I don't do anything on a whim."

"I'm sure you don't. Then how come you have a locked suite of rooms at the ready?"

He sighed, and turned his attention back to his dinner. "It was the original harem."

She raised her eyebrows in indignation. "Harem? What century are we living in?"

"The rooms haven't been used as a harem for many years. But the women in our family continued to use these rooms. Don't you like them?"

"What I don't like is being locked in. Are you saying your women have always been locked in?"

"Of course not. There was no need."

"But there is a need with me."

"Exactly."

"Why?"

He dropped his cutlery onto the plate with a clatter. It didn't seem as if he was going to be given any peace to eat. He made a mental note to eat his dinners alone in future. He steepled his fingers. "Two reasons. One, as I have said, someone appears to have been following you in LA and until I know who and why, it's safest you are protected. Two, I cannot trust you to stay here. I cannot risk you taking away my heir."

"Your heir?" She muttered curse words which made him wince. "My child may be yours," she said quietly, "although I'm not confirming that. But he or she will hardly be your heir. We aren't married."

"Yet," he said, taking a final bite of his meal and standing up.

For the first time, Samantha stood with her mouth open and no words coming out. He rather liked it. He smiled and repeated the word. "*Yet*. But we will be."

She remained immobile as he walked past her and let himself out the door. He took the key, tossed it in the air and pocketed it, without locking the door.

The door was immediately opened with a force which told him she'd expected it to be locked.

"You haven't locked the door!"

37

He turned slowly. "It was simply a precaution, but I believe we have an understanding now. Stay here, I'll protect you and our child and you can have a future of wealth and privilege without fear of whatever it is you're running from. Is it a deal?"

For a moment he wondered if he'd gone too far. He felt something snag inside him. Her eyes were wide and she looked utterly defenseless—just as he knew her to be—and he hated it. Hated to see her vulnerable.

"What choice do I have?" she said, in a hoarse voice which sounded as if it had been forced through a layer of sadness.

He forced himself to be harder. "None," he said, turning away. "Goodnight."

But, as he heard the door close and he continued to walk away from her, his mind didn't leave the room in which he'd just been. He imagined her face, blank with unhappiness and her eyes spilling with tears that he knew she'd refused to allow to fall in his presence. And that face lingered in his mind until long after he'd fallen asleep.

CHAPTER 4

*T*he first thought on Samantha's mind when she awoke was the unbelievable notion that Zeeshan still wished to marry her. However, she didn't feel any panic because, lying in the comfort of the king-size bed with the morning fresh breeze entering through the narrow shutters, she knew it couldn't be true.

True, he'd asked her to marry him and given her the beautiful sapphire ring after only being together a short while. But now? She'd left him without a word. He couldn't really still want to marry her, could he?

She swung her legs over the side of the bed, padded across to the windows and flung them open wide. She was met with softly hazy sunrise and a misty early morning light over the tumble of adobe-colored buildings which marked the edge of the city. Directly before her was the sea, and she instantly felt soothed by its presence.

There was a knock at the door, quiet enough not to disturb her if she'd still been asleep, but loud enough for her to hear if she'd been awake. She opened the door to find a maid standing behind a trolley of hot coffee, rolls and breakfast. She also noticed with annoyance that two men guarded her door. They didn't look at her as she glared at them. She tightened her robe around her. At least the door wasn't locked anymore. At least Zeeshan had listened to her about that.

"That's just what I need," she said with a smile to the maid, who looked surprised at the friendly reception. She opened the door wider. "Come in."

"I'm sorry, madam, I cannot stay. I've been instructed to let you know that your first appointment is in one hour."

Samantha raised an eyebrow. "My first appointment? And who is that with?"

The maid looked embarrassed and shrugged. "His Majesty. I don't know who else who will be attendance. Afterwards, I believe, you have an appointment with the doctor."

"Oh. Anything else?"

The maid looked worried, her smile didn't reach her eyes. "His Majesty asked that you dress appropriately. That you…" The maid hesitated, her eyes looking doubly scared now as she tried to find the right words—presumably *not* the words Zeeshan had used. She swallowed. "That you cover yourself." The maid swept her hand over her stomach and her message became clear.

Samantha's eyebrows shot up. But the maid quickly walked away, no doubt having been instructed not to talk any further than was necessary to Samantha.

Samantha closed the door, placed the tray on a table and plucked a piece of fruit from the plate. She walked back into the bedroom, and flung open the closet wide. There were yet more clothes here, some of them older, more elaborate robes, and some definitely sexier, presumably for bedroom entertainment only.

If Zeeshan thought he could control her every move,

schedule a diary full of appointments without telling her what they were about, and dictate what she should wear, then he had another think coming.

She took a bite of the flat bread, and scanned the wardrobe, her eyes resting on a sequined green dress. It appeared the most unsuitable, the most revealing of her rounded stomach, therefore it would be what she wore. She had nothing to hide and, if Zeeshan did, then so much the worse for him.

As soon as Samantha stepped into his office—half-an-hour before the designated time—she wondered if her decision had been a smart one. Everyone looked up at her entrance. She blinked, knowing the kohl-ringed eyes and bright lipstick and the emerald dress, which didn't stint on the decorative crystals and clung tightly around her pregnant stomach, made her stand out.

Zeeshan's eyes narrowed and he gave a half-sigh through grim lips. The other men in the room gave her an alarmed glance and then fixed their eyes anywhere else, all except one man. Zeeshan shot a warning glare at the man, dismissed the others and beckoned Samantha forward. She walked toward him, making sure she kept her chin held high, and restrained her hands from covering her stomach. She was aware of her high heels clicking on the marble, announcing her arrival in an even less subtle way than her clothes. She'd piled her long hair high on her head in a twisted bun which only emphasized her height. She wanted to come across as a force to be reckoned with and, by the looks on the faces of the retreating men, she'd succeeded.

The man who Zeeshan had allowed to stay rose from his position in an easy chair with a smile. He offered his coffee cup to a maid for re-filling.

"Well, brother," the tall, good-looking man said, "you *have* been busy."

Brother? Samantha's gaze lingered on the handsome man. This must be Adam whom she'd read about. One of Zeeshan's two half-brothers. She didn't think it was the elder one, Rayan, or rather she hoped it wasn't because she'd heard that he'd recently got married. No man should look at a woman the way this man was looking at her if he was married. Despite Adam's single status, it didn't look like Zeeshan was best pleased with Adam's lingering gaze, because he shot him another black look.

"We will talk more of this later, Adam."

Adam shot Zeeshan an amused glance. "I see you want me gone." Adam sent a look to Samantha which could only have been described as appreciative. "And I understand why." He tore his glance back to Zeeshan, whose scowl was even blacker if that were possible. "And I look forward to hearing all about this little situation. Or perhaps *not* so little." Adam sauntered to the door. "Goodbye. I hope we will meet again very soon."

"I hope so, too." She responded to his smile with one of her own, thinking how refreshing it was to meet someone who appeared to like the fact she was here, and liked what he saw. After the door closed behind Adam, she looked around. Zeeshan looked from the closed door back to her with a dark glower.

"If you're quite ready?" he asked, about to turn away.

She reached out and touched his arm, needing his attention. If the clothes didn't do it, then perhaps she had to break down the barrier between them by something more physical. He halted immediately, although her touch had no strength to it, and stared at her.

"The question is, Zeeshan," she said in a low voice, "ready for what?" Despite the thumping of her heart she willed herself to appear cool. She refused to allow him to get the better of her.

She was aware of every inch of her body, of how the dress clung to her curves, which were even more curvy than usual. It was only when she saw him swallow, the kind of swallow which revealed that he was fighting a response which weakened him, that she knew she'd got him. He wanted her, she thought with delight. He still wanted her. He just didn't *want* to want her.

He cleared his throat and the weakness was immediately hidden once more. "Ready to do exactly as I say." He took her hand which was still lightly touching his arm, in both of his hands. She gasped at the feel of his large hands holding hers, emphasizing the fact that he had captured her and wasn't about to let her go. Trouble was, despite her intentions, her body weakened at the knowledge of exactly how thoroughly he was in control of her responses. It was her turn to swallow and to give herself away. A slow, self-satisfied grin spread across his face.

"I see that there is a part of you which enjoys the idea of being held by me, no matter what you say. Perhaps I should come to you later and try to discover the extent of your desire?"

She shook her head but, in response, he tugged her and she stumbled into his arms. He put his other hand out to steady her, his fingers briefly caressing her shoulder before dropping his hand to his side once more. He leaned in close and she could see the lines around his mouth, signifying his self-control, and she could smell his fragrance—leather and ambergris. The kind of fragrance which had made her mouth water when she'd first got close to him, and, it seemed, still had a potent effect on her.

"If you do that you might just find that you get more than you bargained for," she said, irritated to hear her husky tone.

He lifted a lock of her hair from her face. "Ah, now, there you will be wrong. Because I know exactly the bargain I have made." He stepped away, releasing her as he went. "Now, perhaps, we can get down to business."

She had no choice but to follow him to the table. He spoke briefly into the phone before the doors opened and two men entered the room. She was introduced to them and was suddenly on her guard. Why was she having a meeting with Zeeshan and two lawyers? She didn't have to wait long to find out. He introduced her to them as his fiancée.

Suddenly she realized that Zeeshan hadn't been joking about marrying her—far from it.

Zeeshan took his place at the top of the table. She sat to his right, opposite her were the lawyers.

"I think we all know why we are here," said Zeeshan.

"No," she said, folding her arms, refusing to play along with him. How dare he assume she would marry him without asking. "I don't."

A muscle twitched in his jaw. He must be grinding his teeth in annoyance. He heaved a deep sigh, his gaze never leaving hers.

"We are here to discuss our future."

She raised an eyebrow. "Isn't that normally something to be discussed between the two people concerned first?"

There was some clearing of throats and uncomfortable shuffling.

"We *have* discussed it."

She leaned her arms on the table and fixed him with her own stare. "You have told me we will be married. I don't believe in anyone's book that that constitutes a discussion."

He didn't take his eyes off her. "You seem to forget the engagement ring I gave you. You appeared perfectly happy to accept it and all that it implied a few months ago."

"That's in the past. Everything has changed."

"Is that so? Then why, may I ask," he said, leaning forward until he was uncomfortably close to her, "do you still wear the ring?"

"I don't." She stretched out her hand. "Do you see it on me?"

"No. But I know you wear it." Before she could move away, he'd scooped the leather thread from around her neck, exposing the sapphire engagement ring. "I saw it in the photographs taken on the beach in LA, and I saw it while you were sleeping on the plane. You kept it when you had no money." He shrugged. "I can only deduce it's important to you."

She bit her lip, unable to reply. She was infuriated that he'd read her so correctly, frustrated that she was being manipulated quite so effectively. He turned back to the men.

"Gentlemen, perhaps you could leave the paperwork here for me to discuss with Miss Cross. We will reconvene our meeting to make the necessary arrangements later today."

He waited until they'd left the room.

"Make no mistake, Samantha, we will marry. Then, when it is mutually acceptable, we can part. But we *will* marry, and my son *will* be legitimate."

"How can we marry, Zeeshan? We hardly know each other. We don't love each other. It's all so sudden. There's too many other things to think through."

"Like what?"

The silence lengthened as she realized she couldn't tell him exactly how complicated things were. She wouldn't stand a chance at keeping her child then. Marriage or no marriage.

"I thought not. And, as to knowing each other, we know enough to make a child."

She noticed he didn't refute the fact that he didn't love her. "Besides…" She trailed off, knowing she couldn't tell him the real reason. Because once he'd discovered her secret he'd never trust her again.

"Besides what?" he ground out.

"I can't live here." She swept her hand around the room, indicating the world outside. "I don't belong here. And you surely need to marry someone who does?"

"I will marry whoever I need to marry. And I need to marry *you* because in approximately three months' time you will be the mother of my child. *My* child, Samantha. *My* child. And my child will stay with me and be raised by me."

"He's my child, too."

"Of course. And, if it pleases us both, you may remain here, at the palace, as my wife and the mother to my child."

"Remain here captive, you mean."

"I'll do whatever it takes to make this work."

"You can't keep me here, imprisoned like this. I won't have it."

"Of course you won't have it. You like to come and go as you please, don't you, Samantha?" His eyes searched her face. "You like to be around for as long as you want to be and then, for whatever reason, you run away. Just like a scared animal."

He took a step closer and a wave of fear washed over her. "I do not," she remonstrated, except more quietly this time. "I do *not*," she tried to repeat more firmly. It sounded weaker, if anything.

Suddenly his finger rubbed across her lips, coming to rest with a brief caress on her cheek. "Yes, you do. That's what you do, isn't it? Run away. Just as you left me."

His hand hadn't shifted from her face. It was as if he'd forgotten where it was. She shook her head, unable to speak

"You know, I couldn't fathom out why you left in such a hurry, not after the intensity of the months we'd shared." His fingers curled around her jaw and brushed across her throat, caressing lightly. His eyes dropped to her lips—lips which opened despite herself. "Do you remember those nights, Samantha? Do you remember the things we did together?"

She nodded. Of course she remembered, despite her best efforts to forget.

"Do you remember how I made you feel?" He gently felt her pulse. "I can tell by your rapid pulse that you do." He dipped his head and breathed her in, as if she were a flower. His nostrils flared and his eyes darkened. "You were so… responsive to my touch, so ready for me. Was it all a pretense, hey, Samantha?" He tilted her head so she was forced to look at him. And what she saw there didn't reassure her. He looked like he would devour her. It was the same look he'd given when their eyes had first locked across the room.

She mouthed the word 'no'.

His eyes narrowed dangerously. "Tell me, then, what is it you're hiding from me." This was no question. It was a demand.

She tried to shake her head but his fingers held her chin firm. "Tell me," he said, his words vibrating through her. There was a brief moment when she could have spoken, told him everything but, instead, her gaze dipped to his lips which he immediately pressed against hers.

Her whole world changed in that moment. There was no further thought of escaping the room, only of pleading with him to keep her captive for as long as it might take to give her what she needed.

Their tongues and bodies collided. His hands were around her in an instant, gripping her bottom and pulling her against him. The kiss deepened, and for a long moment everything was forgotten. All the anger and hurt and fears dissolved away under the heat of that kiss. Then, as quickly as it had begun, Zeeshan ended it.

Samantha was confused. What was he doing? She knew

he wanted her as much as she wanted him. The kiss had laid that truth bare. Then she heard it—a sharp rap at the door.

He pushed his fingers through her hair and held her head to his, his forehead pressing against hers. "What the hell do you do to me, Samantha? You cast a spell on me whenever you are near. I can't think, I can't—"

The rapping on the door was repeated, for what must have been the third time. He sucked in a deep breath and stepped away. He took another much-needed breath, walked toward the door and opened it wide.

"Good. Please, enter. Miss Cross is ready for you."

Samantha walked to the mirror to give herself time to calm her breathing and to check her hair, which his fingers had teased from the bun. She smoothed it with her trembling hands and turned around with a smile which covered everything she was feeling. Or at least she hoped so. She'd rarely been able to hide what she'd thought and it had always gotten her into trouble.

She glanced at Zeeshan and she could tell from his glance that he wasn't taken in. It seemed Zeeshan could read exactly what was going through her mind. But she sincerely hoped he couldn't read everything because she doubted that, if he knew her secret, he would want anything to do with her.

"I'll leave you," said Zeeshan.

She sighed. "Good morning, doctor. Thank you for coming. I hope it's not an inconvenience."

The door closed and she turned around to find Zeeshan had left the room.

ZEESHAN SWEPT past the guards he'd posted outside the door. She was too precious to leave unguarded. Far too precious— no matter what she might believe. And that kiss only confirmed it. He'd almost forgotten how sweet she was. After she'd left him he'd been consumed by pain, swiftly followed by anger. But all that had vanished the moment his lips had touched hers—a reminder of what they'd once meant to each other.

His footsteps faltered as he remembered the power of those nights of love-making. They'd left an indelible mark on him, on his heart, on his soul and body, and he suspected they had done the same to her. Which, again, begged the question, why did she leave? What, or whose, secrets was she keeping, and why?

She always sidestepped the question, but he'd get the truth from her because their future depended on it. And he knew how. He knew her weakness now—a weakness which was also his.

BY THE TIME the doctor had left, Samantha felt as if a huge weight had been lifted off her shoulders. The baby was progressing well. Her medical appointments had, by necessity, been few. After she'd left Ahmar, she'd stopped off briefly in England. Through her mother, she was a British citizen and so had been able to use the free health system to get a thorough check-up. She'd wanted an amniocentesis test to see if her baby might have inherited cystic fibrosis, the disease which her father had died of, so prematurely. She wouldn't have done anything, she just needed to know.

Fortunately, there were no signs of the disease and so she'd carried on traveling to the US, needing to put as many miles between her and her past life as possible. There, she'd been able to afford only one doctor's appointment. She'd wondered why the doctor had been so insistent on locating her English medical records. Now she knew. Zeeshan had wanted them after he'd discovered she was pregnant.

While it still rankled that Zeeshan had extended his

control over her to the other side of the world, at least she now knew her baby would receive the best care available. The doctor was Zeeshan's own physician and had medical degrees from the best universities in the world. She couldn't be in better hands and that was down to Zeeshan.

She wandered over to the window and looked out, not even thinking about opening the door and going somewhere —where had she wanted to go anyway?

All she had to do was to avoid any situation in which he tried to uncover her secrets, because she was too vulnerable. She knew that, if she were alone with him, it wouldn't be hard for him to get her to open up, whether she wanted to or not. And then, she couldn't bear to imagine how much he'd hate her.

The phone suddenly rang, interrupting her thoughts. She assented to the polite request and then walked away. It seemed she wouldn't be able to avoid her sheikh so easily.

She was late.

The long dining table was set, just as Zeeshan knew Samantha liked it. There was no table cloth to hide the highly-polished dark wood, which contrasted with the shining silver cutlery and the richly decorated dinner service, traditional to Ahmar, in all shades of blue. In the months he'd spent with Samantha, she'd changed his tastes. His parents, and grand-parents before them, had insisted on top-end designer table-ware. But when Samantha had burst into his life, the Versace plates had remained in the cupboard, replaced by the pottery of his people—albeit valuable and rare examples of that pottery. But that was Samantha—warm, extrovert, a person who was interested in people rather than wealth and status.

He glanced at his watch with dissatisfaction. She was also

rarely on time. No one ever made him wait. She was turning his life upside down.

But his irritation was forgotten when the double doors opened and she entered the room. Inside his private quarters, there were no expectations as to how she should dress—western clothes were fine. He'd made sure her wardrobe was full of exquisite clothes. If his beautiful bird had to be kept in a cage, he'd make sure the cage was as fitting as possible. And she did look remarkable in the evening dress she'd selected. Instinctively, he rose to greet her.

The pale turquoise silk fluttered around her body, caught by the evening breeze.

"I wasn't sure you'd come," he said, betraying his fears before he could stop himself. He cleared his throat as she advanced, looking for all the world like a siren from mythology. Her long hair hung loose and flowed around her shoulders, the ends curling around her breasts. It glowed under the flickering candle light.

She walked around to the other side of the table, where a setting had been laid for her. Her gaze swept the table before looking up at him.

"A Bedouin feast," she said dryly. "Are we celebrating some occasion?"

He sighed. This wasn't going to prove easy. "Yes, dinner with you when you tell me the truth."

She grunted and sat down, pulling the chair up roughly beneath her. The scraping sound jarred against the strains of music. She glared at him. "Is there such a thing? One single truth?"

"Of course." He beckoned to the maid to come forward and serve them.

Only when the maid had left the room did she respond.

"You *would* say that," she said, taking a quick sip of the

effervescent water. "I'm sure in your black and white world everything is easy. It's either good, or bad."

"You are correct. Truth is simple."

She shot him another dark look. "No, it's not."

"Perhaps you don't try telling the truth often enough to understand it."

She placed the glass onto the table where it spilt, the drop floating on its highly polished surface. "Ask me a question and I'll tell you the truth."

Her words hung in the air for a moment and he suddenly wasn't sure if he wanted to know the answer.

"Who is after you?"

Her lips pulled into a brief, wry grin. "Start with the difficult one first, why don't you?"

"No," he said. "The difficult one would be 'why did you leave me?' I'm not asking that. I have no interest in that anymore." Lying could be easier than he imagined. "What I want to know is who is after you. My investigations have ruled out the police. Whoever is after you isn't working for the law."

She brought the crystal glass filled with sparkling water to her lips. The bubbles popped in front of her eyes which appeared briefly uncertain, before assuming the air of confidence she'd exuded when she'd first entered the room.

"I don't know." She took a sip of her water and then kept her eyes lowered as she replaced the glass on the table.

"I don't believe you."

She nodded, accepting his statement. "Okay, perhaps it would be more accurate to say I don't know for sure."

He arched an eyebrow in disbelief. "You have so many people after you that you are unsure who it is?"

She bit her lip and he knew that she was prevaricating.

"Samantha," he said firmly. "I'll ask again, because I think you know exactly who it is, but for some reason you're not telling me. That could be because of one of three reasons."

"And what might they be?"

"Either you're protecting them, and that I don't believe because you are too scared of them. Or you are protecting me." He hesitated, waiting to see her reaction. There was none. "Or you are protecting our child." Now she reacted. A blush flowed over her cheeks which never usually betrayed her in this way. She was protecting their baby.

He sat back, satisfied he was on the right track. "You don't need to protect our child. I am quite capable of protecting you both."

Her eyes flared open and she leaned forward. "You don't know these people," she uttered in a hoarse, strained whisper, as if coming from the very depth of her. "You don't know what they can do."

"And you do?" he asked, leaning forward, copying her stance. They were close now and he could see the dark center of her pupil, enlarged with fear.

She grimaced and her lips trembled. He had the irrational impulse to still her lips with a kiss. He gripped his hands into tight balls, to stop himself from reaching out for her. He couldn't weaken just as he was getting somewhere. "And you do?" he repeated. "Tell me what they can do."

She looked up without raising her head. Her face was in shadow apart from the brilliance of her blue eyes. "They know no bounds, Zeeshan." It was the first time he'd heard his name on her lips, and he knew she was telling the truth. Her hand trembled as she curled it around her water glass. She took an unsteady sip, swallowed, and pressed her lips together, no doubt to try to stop them from quivering. "They kill people. They killed my friend, Kirill, when… when he didn't do what they wanted him to do. And they'll kill me, too, and our child."

A surge of adrenalin pulsed through his body at the thought of anything happening to her. "No one will touch you. I can assure you of that."

"You can't keep me here, guarded day and night forever. Apart from anything else, I can't stand to be caged." Her face fell. "I just can't stand it, Zeeshan. I really can't."

Before he knew what he was doing, he'd reached across the table and had taken her hand in his. He didn't know who was more shocked. "You will do whatever you have to do to stay alive. I am here and I'll help you. You have nothing to fear while you are under my protection."

"But you can't hide me away forever." Her eyes glazed with tears, twisting further the knot in his gut.

"I won't have to. I have people investigating this as we speak. All we have to do is to keep you safe while they do their job."

"I can't stay cooped up. It's killing me."

"And I can't let you go, Samantha," said Zeeshan, with an urgency that he needed to convey to her. "If it's as you say, then you're in danger. I think it's time to take you out of the public eye completely."

"What? I'm hardly in it now."

"It's known you are here. And people are coming and going inside the palace too much for my liking. No, I'm going to take you to somewhere even more secure. Somewhere safer."

She shuddered, and for a moment he felt her fear viscerally. But he pushed it to the back of his mind. He had more important things to deal with.

"What place?"

"A castle in the desert."

She narrowed her eyes. "Castle? That sounds positively medieval."

"It's pre-medieval." She nearly choked on her drink. "And it was a prison for many years."

She blanched. He didn't think she could go any paler, but she did. She licked her lips and blinked rapidly as she shakily replaced her fork with a clatter onto the plate.

"Really, Zeeshan?" she said in a choked whisper. "You're going to imprison me?"

"It's for your own good."

She shook her head. "You can't do that. I won't allow it."

He lost his temper and gripped the table. "Then tell me the truth. Give me something I can work with. Tell me why you left me."

"Is that what this is all about?"

"No. You're in danger. But I can't help if you keep secrets from me. Tell me why you left me. I've a feeling it's connected."

"I left you because I couldn't stay in the country any longer." She licked her lips and her eyes strayed, as if she were trying to figure out how much she could say.

"Tell me everything."

She shook her head. "I can't do that."

"Can't or won't?"

"It comes to the same thing. I left the country because I'd made a mistake."

"And can you tell me what this mistake was?"

"You."

He rose, infuriated at her obtuseness. "I'll take you back to your rooms."

"I can find my own way."

"I will take you back to your rooms where you can prepare for your journey tomorrow. I can't trust you, and I can't trust the people who are after you—whoever they are."

They returned to her suite of rooms in stony silence.

She placed her hand on the door. "You're wrong, you know."

"I'm sure I am," he said wearily. "I'm sure you think I'm wrong about everything."

"No. Just one thing. I didn't want to leave you, but I had no choice."

Before he could ask her what she meant, she'd gone in the door, and he heard the key lock inside. His concession. She needed to be locked in but he'd allow her to lock the door.

He walked away. He might not know what she meant. But he would. Because she didn't know it, but he would be accompanying her to the desert fortress. He hadn't planned to, but he'd suddenly changed his mind.

CHAPTER 5

*S*amantha kept her gaze firmly outside the window of the SUV. It felt like they had been traveling for hours, and he still hadn't told her why he felt the need to retreat to a still more secure place. Surely nothing was as secure as the palace? Whatever he knew about the encroaching threat, he wasn't saying. And it made her feel uneasy.

"How much further?" she asked, feeling the distance from the sea acutely.

"Half-an-hour."

She looked around with sudden interest. "Then we should be able to see it, surely?"

He nodded toward the horizon. "If you look straight ahead, you can."

She looked straight ahead and what she saw didn't reassure her. It looked to her like the sands had risen to ninety-degree angles and solidified. The austere walls of the desert castle rose three stories high and were punctured by equally forbidding slit windows, like black marks on a pale yellow canvas. The place was evidently made for defense, not leisure. The central gate was flanked by two semi-octagonal towers. Four more rectangular towers stood at each corner. Now she understood. Nothing, and no one, could get past these walls without invitation.

As they approached she saw signs of what must once have been a large town. Some stone walls still soared straight and true into the blue sky, while others had fallen, and lay scattered across the sand, their jagged outline creating an uneven appearance on the smooth lines of the desert. It must have been a very important complex once. But now, it looked simply like a forbidding refuge surrounded by semi-ruinous buildings.

She ran her finger around the neckline of her top, as a wave of fear and claustrophobia went through her. The last time she'd felt like this was when she'd been eighteen and trapped in a caravan in the middle of nowhere with her unstable mother. The feeling of suffocation, of having to be careful about what she did, what she said, anything that might trigger her mother into doing what she often threatened to do, savagely re-surfaced. Being confined in one space, far from the freedom which the sea represented to her, was her worst nightmare.

She didn't take her eyes off the castle as it slowly increased in size. "You intend to keep me confined here?"

"Yes. For the time being anyway."

"It certainly looks like the prison it once was."

"It was only that for a short time. It's a qasr—a desert castle. Used by my country's rulers for centuries as a place of pleasure and, sometimes, as a refuge from danger."

"And how long do you propose to keep me trapped here, miles from anywhere?" She shifted her gaze back towards Zeeshan and she realized for the first time that his face was equally forbidding. He was part of this world, and she wasn't.

"As long as I have too."

She huffed an exasperated grunt. "That's no answer."

"It's the only answer I can give while you continue to keep secrets from me."

She bit her lip and looked straight ahead. He had a point, but how could she tell him those when the truth could end up separating her from her child?

They drove in silence towards the castle, which grew no more desirable as the details around it became clear. As they approached the looming wall, large dark, battered doors, three times the height of a person, were slowly opened by unseen people, allowing a crack in the otherwise sheer facade.

Only slowing slightly, they drove through the qasr's dark maw into a different world. As the gates closed behind them and the cloud of sand and dust followed them inside, her mouth fell open in amazement. This was no ordinary castle. Within its walls were well-kept buildings, courtyards shaded by billowing canopies, and lush green vegetation.

It was only when she got out of the car she could hear the sound of water. The green was like balm to her eyes and senses. She inhaled the scented air, and listened to the birds which flitted high in the trees above. Everywhere she turned she saw something unexpected—tubs of overflowing greeny-gray herbs beside ancient stone seats, a glimpse of brilliant color as a bird swooped into a tree, and flashes of brightly colored robes as people moved around the buildings.

"This is amazing," she said, turning to Zeeshan, who'd come and stood beside her. She strained her neck trying to take it all in. "Utterly amazing."

"Yes, it's always been this way—a refuge from the desert and the city. Few people outside our borders know it exists. You see, I have not brought you here to suffer, I have brought you here to protect you, to heal you."

She frowned. "I'm not sick."

He sighed as if she were being deliberately obtuse. "Then why do you look so pale, why so strained?"

She looked away and kept her gaze averted. It seemed he could sense exactly how she felt. She felt like a violin whose strings were tightened to breaking point. Not broken yet, but liable to tear apart at any time.

"Things have been..." She paused as she tried to find the right word. There wasn't one. "Hard." It wasn't sufficient to describe what she'd been through, but anything more could be too revealing.

He grunted and looked around. "Then, I trust they will be less *hard* for you here. You'll be safe, here, Samantha. No one can get to you."

No one, except the most dangerous of them all—*you*, she thought. Because she knew Zeeshan had the ability to steal not her body, but her heart and soul.

"Come, I'll show you around."

He took her up to the top of one of the four round towers which rose from each corner of the square castle. From there, they could see all over the castle and surrounding land. It was more extensive than she'd first thought, and virtually impregnable. He pointed beyond the castle wall to where further walled enclosures could be seen. Whatever they'd once been used for, they now lay neglected.

She felt rather than heard him approach her. "It must have been a large settlement once." She frowned. "Seems strange, in the middle of nowhere. Where is the water coming from?"

He pointed behind them to a heavily walled area, set in the foothills leading to a low range of mountains. "Over there are at least five cisterns of which we are aware, and a large reservoir of water. There are sluice gates and water channels which bring the water into the castle. Most of it is underground."

"It sounds amazing."

"It *is* amazing."

"I'd like to see it."

He shook his head, too quickly. "No, there's no point. There's nothing there but stone and water. It's a cold place. Damp and deserted." His gaze lingered a little on the bleak pile of rocks. She looked from him, then back to the rocks.

"You forget, I love the water."

"Not there, you wouldn't. No, I have no wish to revisit it."

"It seems strange that you describe it as something quite incredible, especially for the time in which it was built, and yet you don't wish to show it to me."

He shrugged and turned away with his back to the reservoir. His shoulders were tense. Something about what he'd just described had got to him, and she hadn't a clue what. All she knew was that she'd discovered a chink in his armor and she was determined to find out what lay beneath it.

He cleared his throat and pointed to a wing of the castle below them which appeared to have been newly renovated. "I am more interested in what lies within those buildings. The library here contains a priceless part of my collection of Ahmari literature."

The tension in his shoulders released itself as he continued to focus on the library. She followed his gaze, then looked back at him as she suddenly realized she'd learned something else about him. "You like that place. I mean, you *really* like it."

His expression, too, had softened. "Yes," he said. "Books are important to me."

"Why?"

He shrugged. "An escape, perhaps."

"Escape? That's a funny way of expressing it. You really needed to escape when you had all of this?" She swept her arm around the castle, indicating the obvious luxury.

He held her gaze steady. "Yes, I needed to escape."

She felt she had the upper hand for once. She stepped a little closer to him and was pleased to see his eyes darken with desire. "From what?"

"What?"

She was gratified to see her proximity had made him forget his thoughts. She decided to take pity on him and help him out.

"What were you were escaping from?"

He didn't smile. His face grew serious but his eyes glinted with something she recognized and to which her body responded—sexual desire. He stepped closer to her.

"I'll tell you, if you tell me what *you* are running from."

She licked her lips. He'd got her there. They both had secrets. Her expression must have answered for her.

He grunted. "I thought not. Come on, I'll show you the rest of the castle. And, if you wish it, we will visit our famous hammam."

"Famous baths? Really?"

He raised an eyebrow at her disbelief. "*World* famous."

She followed him down the spiral stone staircase. From the outer courtyard where Zeeshan had parked the car, they entered directly into a large reception hall full of soaring marble columns, which was surrounded by yet more vaulted rooms which appeared to be a mixture of reception rooms. Zeeshan didn't stop in the hall but continued on through to the triple-arched opening through which the central courtyard appeared.

"This is the royal family's private quarters."

Of course it was. It was at the heart of the building, protected on all sides. They walked through until they reached the central point. Samantha knew this because a tall minaret pierced the blue sky. She'd seen it from a distance and could see that the mosque, which it signaled, was positioned central to the castle. "And here is the ancient heart—the Roman buildings."

"It's of Roman origin, then?"

"Indeed. The road upon which we've just driven was an ancient Roman road—a thoroughfare between two major destinations."

"Why didn't it fall into ruin?"

"Because my ancestors decided it could be quite... convenient to disappear from time to time and retreat to such a place. As you can see it has every convenience a king and his family could want." He pointed to one side of the Roman building. "Over there we have the hammam, fed by waters from the reservoir."

He opened the door and she was immediately struck by the light—subdued and mysterious. Sunlight filtered through internal windows, lighting the bright chips of mosaics, the like of which she'd never seen before. Glimpses of naked bodies and limbs caught her eyes as, for some reason the light rippled over the muted colors. She took a step forward and saw why. The baths were extensive and the dark water rippled under a breeze pushed down by a wind catcher, which captured the breeze above the castle and brought it down to cool the air.

"This is..." Words escaped her as she stood looking around.

"One of the wonders of the world." He said stepping beside her. "And it was created by our people."

"How long ago?"

"Around thirteen centuries ago."

She looked at the images on the wall. "I can see now. It's not just people, but animals, too."

"In those day there were plenty of animals to hunt in the desert."

"And flowers." She craned her neck to see higher still.

"Everywhere." She pointed. "And those geometric designs bordering the whole thing. They're fantastic."

"It's even more impressive at night, under candle light."

She swallowed. She couldn't tell what he was thinking in the shadowy, flickering light. "I'd like to see that."

"And what exactly would you like to see?"

"The water, of course." She suddenly felt nervous. "I love the water. Wherever there's water, I want to be. My father used to say I was a water baby. He was never more at home than when on board a boat, and always took me with him. I must have got it from him."

She stopped suddenly, aware that she was talking too much.

"We will return tomorrow, then, if you wish." His voice was gentler than it had been before. She turned around to find him standing close, watching her. "But only if you wish it."

She nodded. "I'd like that."

"So would I." She had the feeling that they were talking about something different from the baths. But before she could backtrack he'd stepped aside. "But, for now," he continued, "I suggest you go to your suite of rooms and make yourself comfortable. I can see you are tired after the journey."

She was surprised he'd noticed. "Sure." Suddenly she wanted to be on her own. Being with Zeeshan had her mind and body in a turmoil, in addition to everything else that was happening in her life. "Sure," she repeated, stronger now. If he wanted her gone, then she was happy to oblige.

He nodded and gave a sharp command. A woman who must have been waiting outside instantly appeared.

"Show Miss Cross to her rooms, please." He turned to her. "I'll see you at dinner."

But, as Samantha followed the woman up a flight of stairs, through room after room, Samantha decided that she wouldn't see him at dinner. Seeing him, being with him, but having this tension and yawning divide between them was too difficult. No, she'd try to keep her distance until he'd left the following day. She had one night to stay away from him before he returned to the city. She could do it.

But, as she was shown the way to her suite of rooms, she realized it wouldn't be as easy as she thought. In order to access her rooms, they had to go through Zeeshan's. It seemed she wasn't going to going anywhere without him knowing. As the maid left her, she closed the door which was all that stood between her and Zeeshan's bedroom, her fingers seeking out the ancient wooden grooves. There was nothing to protect her from him should he choose to open the door. Nothing but an iron latch which slotted loosely into place.

She turned her back to the door. It seemed the women of the ancient palace were protected from everyone except their sheikh. His room lay between hers and the rest of the palace. Only him. And he had access to her at any time. She wondered if he'd come to her. Since they'd left the palace, something had changed between them. They'd both tried to keep up their defenses but she knew they'd dropped. She knew it because she felt naked under his gaze and she wanted to *be* naked under his gaze.

Taking a stuttering breath, she went over to the window and opened the shutter. Her window didn't look out to the desert but down to the inner courtyard. Symbolic, she thought. Keeping the woman inside, safe, trapped. She let the last word linger in her mind, waiting for the usual trigger for her to escape. But it didn't come.

SHE AWOKE MUCH LATER from her afternoon sleep than she'd intended and, for a moment, wondered where she was. Then she remembered, as the pieces fell into place, making a pattern which focused her once more.

She propped herself up on her elbow. Outside the window the world was dark and silent and stars littered the indigo sky. She groped for her phone and saw it was gone midnight. Her sleepless nights and jetlag had caught up with her. She rose and saw someone had laid out dinner on the table and a side light had been turned on. Zeeshan must have given up on her and decided to send dinner up to her.

At least he hadn't come in and demanded her presence. She glanced at the interconnecting door. There was no sound coming from his room. She assumed he must have gone to bed. She sighed and sat up on the side of the bed, and pushed her hands through her hair. She rose, suddenly realizing she was still wearing the same clothes she'd arrived in.

She padded quietly over to the interconnecting door and pressed her ear to the thick wood but she couldn't hear anything. She leaned back against it and thought of Zeeshan lying on the bed behind the door. Her pulse quickened. She closed her eyes tight, willing the unwanted feelings to leave her. But they didn't.

Heat thickened her blood. Slowly, sensuously, she took off her abaya. Under it she wore her jeans which had been left loose under her swollen belly, tied by a sash threaded through the belt loops. She pushed off her jeans along with her knickers, and pulled off her t-shirt and unhooked her bra.

She sighed with delight as the cool desert air caressed her heated skin. She stroked her stomach, thinking of the small baby growing inside her. At first, when she'd discovered she was pregnant, she'd been terrified, remembering the difficult relationship she'd had with her own mother. But she'd never contemplated getting rid of the baby. Her horror had quickly turned to amazement that she should become pregnant so easily. Love for her unborn child swiftly followed. She'd love and adore this child just as her father had cherished her.

Naked, she picked at the food. But the only appetite she had was for something she couldn't have. Something she *shouldn't* have.

So she lay on top of the silken covers, willing the cool night air to rein in her feelings and urges. But, instead, the silk of the bed coverings, their rich colors muted to shades of silver in the moonlight, shifted against her skin, further stimulating her.

She groaned and lay on her side, her hands moving down, from around her belly, to lower, where she felt such intense need. She pressed the palm of her hand against her sex and thought of the man on the other side of the wall. As she moved her hand and her breathing quickened, she remembered the nights they'd spent together and how he had shown such a complete and utter mastery of her body. He'd known what she liked before she did. He'd refused to tell her how he'd acquired such knowledge but, however he had, she hadn't cared, because he'd given her more pleasure than any woman had a right to. And, in the process, had completely spoiled her for anyone else.

He said he only wanted their child, not her. But his kiss had told her otherwise. But still, she could hardly go to him now, demanding satisfaction. She'd have to deal with her pent-up sexual frustration her own way.

She began moving her hand again, pretending that it was his hand, his lips, his cock which entered her. At the thought of how he'd filled her, her breath shortened and she came, her fingers—which had been a poor replacement for him—slipping out from inside of her as her orgasm rocked her body. Perhaps now she could go to sleep.

She rolled onto her other side so she could see out the window. A tall tree grew beside her window, its flickering light creating shifting moonbeams across the rugs on the stone floor. Despite her best efforts, her mind inevitably wandered to Zeeshan. She imagined his body in minute detail from his feet, his calves, and higher. She imagined caressing him, and being connected to him. Her heartbeat quickened and she jumped up. This was ridiculous. She didn't seem to be any cooler, any more satisfied.

All she could think of was the need to cool down, to drive away the heat which just thinking about Zeeshan created deep inside of her. All she could think was that she needed to bathe in the cool, inviting depths of the *hammam* baths she'd seen earlier. She bit her lip. But, of course, she couldn't. For one thing she'd have to pass through Zeeshan's chamber, and, for another… No, that was the only reason she couldn't. But when had she ever let a man stop her from doing what she wanted?

She shook her head and poured herself a glass of water. But the sight of it, sparkling in the moonlight, only made her long to be submerged in water. It seemed an age since she'd done just that. Then, it had been in the sea, before her pregnancy had been too for advanced, and before she'd realized just how determined the Russians were to get hold of her. She hadn't been swimming since. And the rooms she'd rented in the US had barely functioning showers, let alone baths.

Could she? She pressed her ear once more against the door. She hadn't heard Zeeshan come to bed but no doubt he had. It was late and there was no sound, nor light to suggest anyone was still up. In these rooms the floors were made of stone, not wood and so she knew that she wouldn't make a sound. Where was the harm, even if he did catch her?

She refused to think about it. Instead, she plucked a silken robe from the wardrobe and pulled it around her. And without letting herself think any further, she pressed her hands against the door and lifted the latch, inching it up out of its casing, willing it not to make a sound. It didn't. She released a breath, eased the door open, and stepped inside the dark room. There she paused. It was a little lighter in her room where the curtains remained undrawn across the windows. But, in the master bedroom, the moonlight had yet to enter the room, looking as it did across the desert, rather than inward.

She listened to the regular breathing coming from the bed and when she judged it to be safe, stepped quietly across the relative light of the window, toward the farther door. Without pausing she carefully unlocked the door and lifted the latch. There was a clunk as the key engaged and she froze, waiting to hear if she'd disturbed Zeeshan. But his breathing didn't alter and he didn't move. Her eyes could now make out his form on the bed on the far side of the large room. She relaxed. He was still asleep. Without further thought she stepped outside and closed the door behind her.

The part of the castle in which their rooms were located was private, and she proceeded to the hammam without meeting anyone. She crossed the courtyard, pausing to appreciate the scent of the flowers whose perfume was more pungent on the night air, before continuing to the far side of the colonnaded walk and through to the baths.

In the dressing room, she pulled off her robe, glancing briefly at the moonlit frescoes which showed women in various stages of disrobing, before proceeding to what had once been the warm room where the water had been heated. It was no longer heated because it was rarely used, and now the water rose directly from the well, clear and cold. It was just what she yearned for.

Without hesitation she walked up the steps to the side, paused a moment, her hand on her belly, feeling for all the world like one of the sensuous, sexual women portrayed on the walls around her, and stepped into the water. She groaned with pleasure as the cool water flowed around her body and she submerged herself in it, willing it to carry away her body's needs, and her mind's agitation, that just being near Zeeshan again had caused.

She lay, floating on the water, her belly and swollen breasts protruding, pale in the darkness. She immediately relaxed, happy to be in her element once more.

She didn't know how long she lay, allowing the cool water to lap at her body, but it wasn't long enough. Not nearly. Because suddenly she knew she wasn't alone. She froze, still floating, hoping that whoever it was couldn't see her beyond the lip of the pool. Carefully, she adjusted her line of sight but couldn't see anything in the dark. Here, in the water, starlight filtered down from high overhead. She might not see who'd entered, but she was damned sure she would be fully visible to them.

She dropped to her feet quietly and looked around. It wasn't until her second sweeping glance that she saw him.

"Zeeshan," she whispered, the water dripping off her breasts and stomach as she stood there, unable to move. He stood looking at her for one, long moment before he cursed under his breath and pulled off his robe.

CHAPTER 6

$\mathcal{A}$s he came closer to her, the light revealed what her eyes were hungry for—his body. He was tall, with broad shoulders and chest, and well-muscled limbs. But that was all a frame for what she stared at. His cock was fully erect, and she couldn't take her eyes off it. It was all she wanted. A shiver ran through her body, settling in her sex, which throbbed with need.

He stepped into the water and stopped short of her.

"You are so beautiful," he murmured. "Like a siren who has risen from the water to cast a spell on a man."

She didn't smile back, or refute what he said, because she felt exactly that. She thought, in that moment, that anything was within her power. She raised her hand to his. He took it and she tugged him toward her, aware that there was still a reluctance inside of him, despite what his body wanted. She didn't care about that reluctance now. She wanted it gone. Because she knew it was all that stood between her and mind-blowing pleasure.

She closed her eyes as, with the back of his fingers, he

touched her breast, as gently as the water lapping around her hips. She swayed as his fingers played with her nipples which were fully extended, as if ready to give nourishment, except it was too soon for that. They were for him, and for pleasure only.

She felt a corresponding tug inside of her as he cupped both her breasts and bent down and placed his mouth first over one and then the other. She slid her fingers into his hair as the wet heat enveloped her, and she tilted her hips towards him, wanting everything he could give her.

She panted as he nearly brought her to orgasm with her breasts alone, but he stopped before she came. He caressed her stomach with such tenderness that she nearly wept. She stepped into his arms, pressing her belly and breasts against his hard body, feeling safe within his arms as they encircled her. Then he pressed his lips against hers in a kiss which made her forget everything, except her need for him to be inside her.

She writhed against him as their tongues tangled, taking his cock in her hand, cupping her palm along its silken length. He put his hand over hers and pulled her away. With a brief kiss, he lifted her into his arms and waded through the water to where it was shallower and there were areas designed for reclining. He set her to standing but before he could kiss her again she turned around in his arms and, before he could do anything, she pushed out her bottom until it collided with his cock. She knew how she wanted it.

She leaned forward until she could hold onto the side. He eased her hips up, angled them and then slid inside her. She cried out with the utter bliss of it. All she could think of was one repetitive thought—she'd missed him, she'd missed him, oh, how she'd missed him. She'd missed the intimacy with him, the joy he gave her and something more which she'd never before been able to explain—but now she could—she'd missed the love they felt for each other. It was a part of them both and she didn't know how she'd managed to deny it for so long.

He withdrew and then pushed inside her again, holding her in exactly the right position to give her maximum satisfaction. As if that weren't enough, he put one hand under her breast, playing with her extremely sensitive nipple, while he used the other one to play with her clitoris. She didn't stand a chance.

It took six thrusts to come the first time, with an explosive cry which rang out around the hammam. The water roiled around them as, with a few more thrusts, Zeeshan cried out and pumped his seed inside of her.

Samantha opened her eyes to see the naked bodies and ecstatic expressions of the people painted on the wall. Other vignettes showed people watching. It was as if they were alive and watching her. It should have freaked her out, but, instead, it made her feel intensely desirable, intensely turned on.

They rolled onto their sides, the water lapping at their bodies. They kissed with all the tenderness that she knew he contained behind that fierce facade.

"What am I to do with you, *habibti?*" he asked in a half-groan, half-whisper against her ear. "You have bewitched me. I can think of nothing else but you, and what I wish to do to you."

She closed her eyes and exhaled a sigh of relief. She kissed his cheek and then stroked it. "It's the same with me. I crave you, Zeeshan. You're like a drug, something my body needs. Sometimes I wish I'd never met you."

He propped his head on his elbow and looked down at her, while, with his other hand, he traced the outline of her hip, drawing around her waist before trailing across her breasts. She sucked in a harsh breath as he lightly grazed her nipple.

"But you *have* met me, and our fates are now entwined." He held her a little tighter, as if he was never going to let her go.

She swore lightly under her breath. "What the hell are we going to do about it, Zeeshan? We're bound together, but we're still strangers with secrets. How is there any kind of satisfactory future in that for either of us?"

"How?" He pushed back a stray lock of her hair from her face. "That is down to us. We have to move forward, we have to find out how to make this work. We have no other choice."

"But what if we don't?"

"Then our future will be, at the best, unsatisfactory."

"And at the worst?"

He stopped stroking her back. "That, Sammie, depends on the secrets." She couldn't prevent a shudder from rippling through her body, and his gaze intensified.

"It could mean deep unhappiness for us all," she said.

"And yet, surely, if they are not revealed it will also bring us great unhappiness?" he said softly. "And you'd really risk that, for our child?"

"I'd risk anything for my child."

He stood up and stretched out his hand to her. "Come, let's go to bed. We'll talk of this in the morning."

Reluctantly, she rose from the cool water and stepped up to him. He placed her robe around her before pulling on his own robe. At the door he glanced back at the baths. "I should have known you'd be at home here. You almost make me feel that I belong."

She frowned at his words but had no opportunity to ask him what he meant before they'd left the hammam and she was overwhelmed by the beauty of the gardens at night. The night insects hummed and nocturnal birds cried out, annoyed at their intrusion. And there was always the sound of water. It was a place designed for the senses. Despite that, she had no desire to linger. The imperative of his hand pulling her toward his bedroom was all she could focus on.

Once inside his room, he closed the door and pushed her robe from her shoulders, dropping kisses onto her throat, her collarbone and then lower. She tilted her head back, looking up at the moonbeams which played across the dark, oak-beamed ceiling as she surrendered herself to sheer, unadulterated pleasure.

ZEESHAN LAY CLOSE TO HER, looking at her face as she snuggled into his arms. She'd been fast asleep but, as dawn broke around them and the dim light had crept slowly into the room, she'd suddenly become restless. He'd been marveling at her beauty and at how relaxed she was in sleep. He could almost imagine that there was nothing between them—no misunderstandings, no secrets—nothing to prevent their deep connection which could no longer be denied. And then, as the room lightened toward morning, she frowned and her eyelids flickered with activity. She moaned and moved her head from side to side. He brought her closer, trying to comfort her from the unknown images which were filling her dreams, but still she whimpered and shifted in his arms.

He tightened his grip. "It's all right, *habibti*. It's only a dream."

Then she struggled further and tried to free herself.

"Sammie, wake up! Wake up, you're dreaming."

Her eyes snapped open and he thought his heart would break at what he saw there—sheer terror.

"Sammie! What is it?"

Her name seemed to break the spell and he could see

he'd gotten through to her. The terror slowly ebbed from her eyes and she rolled on her back so he could no longer hold her gaze. She swallowed and he leaned over her, caressing her cheek. "You must tell me. What were you dreaming of?"

She sucked in another breath and then rolled her head on the pillow so she was looking at him once more. A soft smile played on her lips. "Why? Will you make it go away?"

He kissed her. "I'll try. I cannot bear to see you so distressed."

She took the hand which caressed her face and kissed it, before placing it on her full breast. He couldn't help himself. He splayed his fingers and played with her nipple. She wriggled with pleasure under his ministrations. He frowned.

"You are trying to distract me," he growled.

She glanced down at where he was hardening by the second, and raised an eyebrow. "And it looks like I'm succeeding."

He struggled, but only for a second, before grabbing her and rolling onto his back, taking her with him. She sat astride his hips, looking for all the world like a Goddess of utter temptation. "For now. But we will come back to this, Samantha."

"I see I'm back to Samantha." She took hold of him in both her hands. "I can see I'm going to have to work at being your Sammie again."

"I think that's a very good idea," he said, lying back as she positioned herself over him, before sinking down onto him.

He gasped as he was filled with such an intensity of feeling that, for a moment, his mind blanked out and all he was aware of was sensation. She lifted herself up and then sank down on him, her eyelids fluttering again now, not because of distress, but because she, too, was filled with pleasure. She touched herself as she repeated the movement, and her full breasts with dark, peaked nipples swung in front of him.

It didn't take long before he felt the effects of her orgasm, massaging him, as if trying to get every drop of him out. He obliged with a firm grunt.

She leaned over, brushing her breasts against his chest, and kissed him. But before he could capture her in his arms and kiss her thoroughly, she laughed and escaped him.

"Come back to bed," he growled. "I wish to talk to you."

She raised an eyebrow. "Do you, indeed? Well," she said, backing away and plucking her robe from the chaise at the foot of the bed, "I'm afraid you're out of luck."

He got up and stepped towards her. She was tall, but she still appeared delicate next to him. "Luck hasn't anything to do with it," he said as he reached out and grabbed her hand and drew her to him. "Now, Samantha, am I going to get what I want from you?"

"Depends what you want."

"I want to know why you awoke from your dreams in such distress. It's not the first time. What is it that's worrying you?"

She blinked lightly and looked away, her lips twisting into a grimace. "Okay, I will tell you. But, first, let me shower, yes?" There was no way he could deny her anything. He suspected she knew that.

"Okay. But I will come into the shower with you, just to make sure you don't slip away."

He did. And she didn't.

BY THE TIME they emerged from the bedroom suite, food had been laid out for them in the dining room. Samantha thought she could get used to this. Sheer pleasure in bed, and all her needs catered for. Except, she remembered with a frown, the fact she was practically imprisoned. And she had secrets, which she knew, if they ever came to light, would undermine her shaky relationship with Zeeshan.

With some fruit in her hand, she stood by the open door and looked out at the beautiful morning with the sunlight flickering down from between the shades and ferns to the fountain in the middle of the courtyard, and the fragrant blossoms nodding in the gentle breeze. It was the perfect temperature, the perfect place, or it would have been, if she knew she wouldn't be thrown out of here as soon as Zeeshan knew the truth about her and the men who wanted her.

"You look thoughtful," Zeeshan said, standing beside her, taking a sip of his coffee.

She straightened up and smiled, forcing the thoughts to the back of her mind. "Just wondering why you haven't left yet."

"I've decided to delay my trip. There's nothing I can't do here, remotely, at least for the next few days. Besides, you haven't yet told me what it is I want to know."

She opened her eyes wide, feigning innocence. "And what might that be?"

His eyes narrowed in warning. "You know. You avoided telling me earlier, but not now. I want to know what it is which troubles you night after night."

She grimaced and pushed herself off the door jamb, and walked into the room, turning her back on the glorious day.

"It happened on a day very different to this." She paused and glanced around at him. He seemed to be waiting for her to continue. She drew in a calming breath. She could do this. She could tell this man the thing she'd never told anyone.

"Go on," he said, in a patient, encouraging tone.

She began to pace the room. It felt easier that way. "It was raining. We—that is my parents and I—were on the west coast of New Zealand's South Island. We lived in a caravan—

a kind of hippy lifestyle—always moving on. My father did odd jobs and my mother was an artist. Well, ever since we'd arrived there, it had rained, heavily. Day after day of rain, and our caravan was parked up in the bush. Nothing but dark green, dripping leaves above, and mud underfoot. It was as if a cloak of gloom had fallen over us and we were all in bad moods. Dad was walking on eggshells with Mum. I didn't realize why, but I was beginning to. From time to time Mum would disappear. My father invented excuses to cover up for her. It was only much later that I discovered she'd checked into a mental health facility. Bi-polar some called it, undiagnosed schizophrenia." She shrugged. "I don't know what it was. But it had gotten worse ever since we'd arrived on the rainy west coast."

She stopped pacing, took a sip of water and sat down. She'd hoped the growing tension inside her would ease. But instead it worsened. She put her head in her hands, pressing her fingers to her skull as if it would make the words come out easier, as if it would take away the hurt. Tears sprang from nowhere and she kept her gaze averted. She swallowed and wiped her face on her sleeve, hoping Zeeshan wouldn't see.

"Sammie," he said softly. "Go on."

She looked up to find him standing closer. "Dad died. It felt sudden at the time because I'd been ignoring the signs. He had cystic fibrosis and had gradually become weaker. Then he got a cold, which turned into pneumonia from which he was too weak to recover. Mum went to pieces. It tipped her over the edge and from that day on we were stuck together in the caravan, Mum in her madness, and me, trying to stop her taking her own life." She shrugged. "It worked for a while, but one day she walked out into the rain and didn't come back." She swallowed. "I found her the next morning..." She couldn't go on. "I'll spare you the details." She looked away, unable to hold his gaze, wondering what he was going to do with this knowledge. Apart from the grief, she also felt deeply guilty that she'd been unable to prevent the deaths of her parents. "My nightmares vary. Sometimes it's how Dad looked when they pulled back the sheet. Other times it's the rainforest and how I... found Mum."

She heard Zeeshan swear under his breath in Arabic, words she had never heard him say before. Then he was beside her, pulling her tight against him, pressing his lips to the top of her head.

"I'm sorry, Sammie, so sorry, you had to endure such a thing. No one should."

She swallowed, swiped at her tears and pulled away, forcing a smile on her face. "I survived. I'm not the only person who has suffered in one way or another, and I won't be the last. Unfortunately." She bit her lip, willing herself not to break down. She hated sympathy. She jumped up, needing to put some distance between them in order to think clearly. "I can't do this, Zeeshan."

His eyes narrowed and he shook his head in confusion. "Do what? Tell me." He took a step towards her, narrowing the distance she needed. She took another step away. "Tell me what other things are troubling you. I need to know everything."

She shook her head, as she tried to figure out how to hide from him that this wasn't her only secret. She turned away. "I can't do this," she repeated. She tried to walk away but he grabbed at her hand. "Please, Zeeshan, I said I can't do this."

"You've already done it. You've told me something which is at the heart of you. Something which explains why you cannot bear to feel trapped, why you have a need to be free which is beyond the rational. I understand now."

"Understanding isn't everything."

"Yes, it is."

She jutted her chin up in defiance. She felt cornered but she'd come out fighting. "Fine. Then, if understanding is everything, I suggest you repay the favor."

He narrowed his eyes.

"I suggest you tell me what it is that's haunting you. Tell me why you won't take me to what is meant to be one of the seven wonders of the world—the underground reservoir. You have secrets too and, if we are to have any kind of future together, you need to help me understand you."

A muscle flickered in his jaw and she felt a sense of relief. Somehow she'd managed to turn the tables, to deflect his interest from her. All his energies now were going into defending himself, protecting his secrets.

"It's your turn, Zeeshan," she said softly, in a tone that was barely above a whisper.

The last remaining barriers that lay between them fell instantly. It seemed that she could get to him more with *how* she spoke, rather than the words she spoke. She wasn't surprised. She'd come to realize that their bodies instinctively responded to each other—beyond intellect, beyond reasoning—at a primitive level which couldn't be denied.

He nodded and gave a sad smile. "In the interests of mutual comprehension, I will show you something... a place which haunts me to this day."

She smiled. "Thank you. Is it what I imagined it to be?"

"Yes." He walked over to the window and pointed out, beyond the courtyard, to the scattered buildings which were all that could be seen of the ancient system of reservoirs.

"What I found there, hidden in the foothills, changed me forever." He turned to her with a sigh. "I have told no one about this, only those who were there know. I cannot believe I am telling you."

"I'm not just someone passing through, Zeeshan. I'm

going to be your wife, the mother of your child. It's important to share things if we're going to move forward."

"Of course."

But there was something in the way he said it, something in his eyes, which made her wonder whether he, like her, was still keeping secrets.

CHAPTER 7

*S*amantha had to wait until the sun had lost its heat before they set out for the reservoir complex. While Zeeshan worked in the more modern office suite, she spent the day reading, walking around the castle, and swimming in the bathing pool, which was adjacent to the hammam baths in which they'd made love the night before.

She felt as if she were in another world—a world insulated from the problems she'd been living with day in, day out, for the past three months. Problems which had consumed her and frightened her. It was a relief to feel safe again, even if it was an illusion. She knew, at some point, Zeeshan would discover who was after her and why. But, until that time, she'd enjoy the luxury and safety of her surroundings, if only for her baby's sake.

And, maybe, if she managed to discover Zeeshan's secrets, she would be able to weather the storm when her own secrets were uncovered. She had to get closer to him. She had to make him love her as she loved him. Only then would she possibly stand a chance when he knew the truth.

At the appointed hour, she was waiting for him by the

fountain when she sensed, rather than saw him. She felt a prickle track down her spine, coming to rest low inside her. She smiled to herself at their connection before turning slowly around, instinctively allowing her robes to drape around her, showing off her figure, exactly as she knew he liked it.

He stood at the entrance to the garden looking at her. His eyes trailed lazily up her body until they met her own. He greeted her with a sensuous smile of his own.

"You look as if you are in a painting. A heroine from long ago, maybe?"

"A heroine? What kind, I wonder. A warrior woman, a romantic woman, or—"

"A seductress, awaiting her lover."

"Ah, yes." Her grin broadened as she walked over to him and touched him, her fingers smoothing up his arm before gripping him firmly. "However, I think you'll find I'm real enough."

"A *real* seductress." He gave a half-laugh, as he captured her hand in his own. "That's exactly the kind of seductress I like."

"Really?" She cocked her head to one side. "I didn't realize you had different kinds of seductresses in your life."

"I have only one. You." He lifted her chin and pressed his lips to hers. She sighed as he, too quickly, pulled away. "And, as much as I'd like you to seduce me now, we'd never leave the castle."

"Um," she said, smoothing her finger over her bottom lip, watching with pleasure as his eyes traced the movement of her finger. "I'm beginning to think that might not be such a bad idea."

He shrugged. "It's your decision. It was you who wanted to visit the underground cisterns."

She grimaced, trying to pull herself together, out of this

lethargy of sensuality. She sighed and nodded. "Yes, I did. I'd like to see such a wonder of the world. Even if it has such a prosaic name." She didn't say that what she'd was most looking forward to was figuring out what the place meant to him. He was hiding something, and she was determined to find out what.

He stood aside to allow her to exit the garden. "Then we should go before it gets too late."

It only took five minutes to arrive at the foothills in which the reservoir system was hidden.

Zeeshan helped Samantha out of the car and she held on to him for a moment, feeling faint and hot under the still-strong sun.

"Are you all right?" he said, concern etched in his face. "Is it too hot for you?"

"I'll be fine," she said, hoping she was. She looked around. "So long as we don't have to walk far?"

He shook his head. "The entrance to the complex is only a few minutes away."

She took up his offer of an arm for support and they walked carefully through the shifting sands.

"How come such an important complex is so hidden?" She gestured to the desolate landscape, no sign of habitation.

"It's hidden for two reasons. One from the sun, to preserve the water more effectively. The other, from enemies, because it was the lifeblood of our ancestors' civilization."

They entered the twisting passageway, alongside which orange-hued granite slabs rose high into the bright blue sky. Within the confines of the narrow path, all was quiet. A few minutes in, Zeeshan stopped and nodded overhead. "This is where the guards would attack unwanted intruders."

A shiver ran down her spine. He caught her look briefly before moving onwards. It seemed he, too, felt uneasy.

He stopped at an ancient door which blocked their way. He withdrew a large, old-fashioned key and unlocked the door. It creaked heavily, and they entered what looked to be a cave, with a shower of dust and sand.

She was immediately struck by the change in atmosphere. From the dry heat of the desert, she felt the presence of water. The air was damp and cool.

"This way. Be careful. It can be slippery inside."

She took hold of his hand and he led her along the narrow passage. She suddenly felt nervous. He must have sensed it because he turned around and smiled at her. "You'll have to trust me, Sammie."

"I do," she replied without hesitation.

"Good." He stepped ahead of her and suddenly they'd arrived.

"This is amazing." She turned 360 degrees, absorbing the atmosphere of the place. "It's like a cathedral to water! Who'd have thought it was here?"

"Indeed. That is the whole idea."

"But how come? Is it fed by a spring?"

He shook his head. "No. It's fed by water collected from the mountains. You remember the strange shaped rocks on the ledges?" She nodded. "They collect any rainwater and feed it into these underground cisterns, of which this is the largest."

"There are more?"

"Yes. Many more which once supported a large civilization." He knocked the side of the wall. "The water is prevented from seeping into the earth by waterproof cement."

"Cement? So it's modern?" She was confused.

"No. It's the work of the Nabateans when they created the ancient civilization of Petra." He shot her a wry glance.

"When people in your world were still savages, hunting and gathering."

"Okay," she said, with a grin. "I get it." She shrugged. "I guess we just see desert now and assume—"

"Assume that nothing exists here, and nothing has ever existed here of consequence," he said, finishing her sentence, knowing exactly what some western people assumed about his civilization.

She grunted in assent, uncomfortable at her naiveté.

He looked around. "People also used to live here in times of crisis. And sometimes, were held here against their will."

"And so, what does this all have to do with you, and your secret?"

"Come, I will show you."

He led her further into the hillside. Eventually he stopped in a small, dark cave far away from the main reservoir. "It was here I found my mother." He shrugged. "I suppose she thought it would be the last place anyone would come looking for her. No one ever came here. There was no need."

"Found your mother? What on earth was she doing here?" She turned to look at Zeeshan, whose face had assumed an unhealthy pallor in the weird, dim light.

He looked at her, his eyes also devoid of color, empty of everything now. He grunted dismissively, as if unwilling to talk about it. "She was with a friend."

"A friend?"

"The kind of friend, Sammie, whom she did not want her husband, my father, to know about."

She swore under her breath. "Oh, I see!" Then wondered if she did see, because it was so scandalous. "Or at least I think I see."

"I'm sure your first guess was correct. She was terrified of my father, with good reason."

"And yet she was…" She trailed off, unwilling to spell out what Zeeshan hadn't yet.

"And yet she was having an affair with the sheikh of the local area."

"So what happened next? Did she see you?"

"It was he who saw me first. I was young, seven years of age, and couldn't believe what I was seeing. So I stood there, watching my mother writhe and moan in the arms of a stranger. But it was this stranger who saw me and called out to me."

"Oh my God. What happened next?"

"I ran away. I couldn't get away fast enough."

"And later?"

"Later, my mother never said a word to me about it, but he did. The man I saw her with."

"What happened?"

"My mother's lover waited for me and caught up with me and had a 'man to man' talk. He told me that if I loved my mother I must never breathe a word of what I'd seen." Zeeshan gestured helplessly with his hands. "As if I would. I wasn't that stupid. By that time, I knew what my father was like."

"What was he like?"

Zeeshan blinked, as if unwilling to describe his father. She could sense his unease and she reached out and touched his shoulder. He turned to her his eyes full of hurt. "My father was evil."

Her eyes shot open wide. "Evil?"

"Yes. He did many evil things, and my brothers are scared now of only one thing."

"And that is?"

"Of having the same genetic code as our father in their veins, of becoming like him. That is why…" He trailed off.

"Why what?"

"Never mind."

"And you? Aren't you also scared of that?"

"No, I'm not." He held her gaze steadily as if he wanted her to understand something, but she didn't have a clue what.

She suddenly grabbed her pregnant stomach. "Oh, no! What if…" She didn't finish her sentence, unable to put into words the appalling fear that her unborn child might inherit those same genes. She opened her mouth to speak, but how could she wonder out loud if her child would have the potential to be a monster like his grandfather? He must have read her mind.

"And you mustn't worry, either." Before she could ask him what he meant, he'd carried on. "Anyway, my mother didn't dare ask for a divorce. She knew it would result in the death of both her and her lover."

"Surely not!"

"You don't know my culture. It can be unforgiving when the ruler is cruel, when her husband was king. Even more especially when her husband was a cruel misogynist, who would never forgive such a slur to his manhood."

"So, what happened? Did she finish her brief affair and return to your father?"

He held her gaze but she couldn't read him. "It wasn't a brief affair," he said eventually.

She opened her eyes wide. "You mean she risked everything to continue it?"

"No. He ended it, knowing the risk was too great after I'd discovered their secret. He left the country, left his family and his life. What I mean is that she'd been having an affair with him for many years before I found out."

"You must have been devastated."

"I couldn't believe my mother had done such a thing. I knew what my father was like but still, she'd raised me to be ethical, to be good, strong, to trust people, and not to deceive. And then, suddenly it seemed my mother was none of these things. Truth and trust is important to me, Sammie, because of it. Very few people know about this, but I can trust you, can't I?"

"Yes, you can. I know it might look as if you can't because of what happened. But that's behind me now."

"Are you sure?"

She nodded and he picked up her hand and kissed it, and cradled it between his. "Good. Let's get out of here."

EVEN THE DARK of twilight seemed light to Zeeshan as he stepped out of the tunnel, helping Samantha up after him.

But he'd left something behind which he hadn't anticipated. In delving into the dark of his and his mother's past, he'd somehow left something of the dark in his soul behind. The memories associated with the place—of betrayal and someone diminishing before your eyes—which had haunted him for years, had gone. He felt lighter.

Samantha turned around from looking out across the desert to the horizon. She looked at him with such an expression of trust in her eyes that he walked up to her, cupped her face and kissed her.

"What's that for?" she asked, with a smile.

"For making me come here, for being here with me."

"I could see that the place haunted you for some reason. I had no idea that it was where your whole world must have fallen apart. Things like that leave their mark on a person."

"Yes, it certainly did. But the mark only deepened a few years later."

"Why, what happened?"

"My mother died. But, just before she passed away, she opened up about her affair. She said he had been the love of her life. I felt torn between my parents. I had been raised to put duty before anything else and that my mother hadn't? It appalled me."

"What happened to your mother's lover? You said he left the country. Did you ever see or hear of him again? Did he come to your mother's funeral?"

"No. He died ten years ago, in an accident in the rain forest in South America. He'd been traveling ever since he'd left my mother, moving from one place to another, never stopping. It was a freak accident, apparently."

He could see confusion in her eyes. "How do you know so much about him?"

"You asked me if I was scared of being like my father and I replied that I wasn't."

"Why was that?"

"Because my father wasn't my birth father. He is not a blood relative of mine."

She stopped walking, opened her mouth, and just gaped at him.

"My birth father was the man I saw only twice—once in the reservoir cave where he was making love to my mother, and once when he came to swear me to secrecy. That is why I am not scared of becoming a monster like my father. And that is why my brothers agree I should be king. Legally, either one of them could appeal as I am not a blood son. But they won't. And that, Samantha, is my greatest secret, now told to you. I'm trusting you not only with the secret, but with the future of the kingdom. It could be jeopardized if the truth is known, especially by my enemies. And my country cannot be weak, especially now. Do you understand?"

She nodded. "Why? Why would you trust me with so much? I mean, I'll never tell anyone, and you can totally trust me. I just wondered, why now?"

"Because you deserve to know. You are, after all, carrying

our child and you need to know that he cannot inherit the genes of my father, the old king. It's an impossibility."

He didn't know if he'd made the biggest mistake of his life, or had made the best decision in his life. Time would tell. Truth was, it felt good to trust someone at last, someone other than his two half-brothers. There was always the undercurrent of the knowledge that he was king at their behest, simply because they didn't trust themselves, only him.

He grunted. Trust. It was key to everything in his life. And he felt enormously relieved that he'd expressed his trust in Samantha. His feelings for her ran deep, more than the sum of his thoughts and willpower, so it was a relief to know that he trusted her. Yes, she had disappeared from his life suddenly, but he knew that something had made her leave, and that something had nothing to do with her feelings for him because he knew, now, that they were a mirror of his own. They were meant to be together.

No, whatever had made Samantha run away was an external threat, and as such was far easier to hunt down and exterminate, and he'd do exactly that.

What had lightened his step was the thought that things might be okay. He felt that maybe he could trust her with anything, even his future.

ONCE BACK INSIDE the desert castle, they parted ways. He'd been spending too much time out of the office and he'd been told someone had been ringing him endlessly.

But still their parting was difficult. He kissed her, and she pressed close against him. "Can't you come with me now?" she asked, with the prettiest smile and simmering look, which had him desperately wanting to do as she said. He knew she'd make it worth his while. But his phone buzzed just in time to keep him on track.

"No, Sammie. Why don't you go and rest, preserve your energy, and I will return as soon as I've finished my work."

"Okay, then," she said, reaching up on tiptoes and pressing her full lips to his. Her mouth opened up like a flower under his. He lightly touched her tongue and felt her moan vibrate through his body. He pulled away with a deep breath, wanting to inhale every inch of her, from her own sexy smell to the light perfume in her hair.

"I must go."

She smiled, the kind of sultry smile of a woman who knew she'd captured the full attention of her man. "Don't be long." She took his hand and brazenly placed it, palm down, against her sex. "I want you here, Zeeshan." Before he could change his mind, she turned and he watched her leave the room. Her curvy body grazed the sides of her abaya, as she walked that sexy, swaying walk, away from him.

He willed his erection to fade and walked swiftly to the office, glad that he wasn't encumbered by the tight clothes of his western counterparts.

As soon as he entered his office the phone rang. "Who is it?" he asked his assistant as he walked past. The man frowned. "He wouldn't say. All he said was that it was personal and he'd speak only to you. But he said enough to convince us that he knew you. Plus, you'd paid some of his bills in the past few months."

"Ah," said Zeeshan, suddenly realizing who the mystery caller might be. He'd paid off the private investigator he'd hired to find Samantha. Maybe he was after more work.

He flicked the phone over to the computer screen so he had a video connection, too, as soon as his assistant had left the room.

"What's so urgent? You've done your job and been paid as we'd agreed."

The grizzled American detective who wouldn't have stood out in a crowd looked uncharacteristically concerned. His heavy brow was lower than Zeeshan had ever seen it. "I've been approached by someone wanting to find someone."

"Do they know of our connection?"

"I don't believe so. It was from a colleague. We share information sometimes."

"And what's so important about this information? After all, I have what I wanted."

The man was silent for a few moments, which made Zeeshan nervous. His heart thumped. "Are you alone?" asked the man. "Is this a secure line?"

"Yes." Zeeshan's frown deepened. "What's this about?"

"Samantha Cross. You know, of course, that you weren't the only one looking for her."

"Of course. That is why I brought her here, to be safe until we can identify the threat."

"Well, I can help you there."

Zeeshan felt a feeling he was unfamiliar with—a crawling feeling low in his gut like a worm was eating at his insides —fear.

"I don't know what Samantha Cross has done, but she's got the Russian Intelligence Agency on her back. They want her, and they're prepared to do anything to get to her."

Zeeshan closed his eyes tight and gripped the back of the chair, as his mind filled with horror. He was failing at the one thing which guided his life—protecting those he loved, and his people.

"Are you still there, Your Majesty?"

He drew in a deep breath and released his hold of the chair. "Yes, I'm still here."

"What would you like us to do?"

"Do? What options do we have? We can't smash the Russians, and we can't outrun them, the only thing we can do is to understand why they want her."

"Oh, we know that."

"Then tell me," Zeeshan said between gritted teeth.

"They don't like it when they pay people to do something and that something isn't done."

"They paid her to do something? What?"

"Seduce you."

CHAPTER 8

"Seduce me?" Blood pounded in Zeeshan's temples, confusing his thoughts, obscuring the truth. What the hell was going on? Had he heard correctly?

"Yes, that night, six months ago when she appeared as if out of nowhere, you said?"

"Yes."

"Well, you were right. She *had* come out of nowhere, specifically to seduce you."

Zeeshan closed his eyes as Samantha's beautiful face filled his mind's eye. He couldn't believe it. Then he remembered how he'd seen her first on the beach and had been immediately attracted to her, but had retreated, despite her wide smiles and inviting figure. He didn't usually indulge himself in casual sexual encounters and he'd walked away. Then he'd noticed her in a club, partying with friends. Again, he'd walked away. But then, she'd appeared out of the blue, at a royal reception held in one of his hotels. She hadn't been on the invitation list—he'd checked—but had managed to gain entrance to the party anyway. Any suspicions over her presence had been obliterated by his desire for her. But now those initial suspicions arose once more, confirming his PI's story. Samantha had received help in gaining access to him. It hadn't been his lucky day after all.

"But why?" Zeeshan jumped up and paced the room, keeping an eye on the computer as he went. "No, you must have it wrong. It doesn't make sense. Why could seducing me possibly help my enemies?"

"Not in itself, sure," said the PI. "But when she's told to seduce you at a derelict port building, well, then it becomes the kind of opportunity that your enemies don't get every day."

"An opportunity to kidnap a king," Zeeshan said softly. Each word drove the truth harder, like a knife into his gut.

After all his talk of trust, Samantha had betrayed him, at the very beginning of their relationship. He remembered how she'd tried to persuade him to go to a nearby building at the port where she said she was staying. She'd said they would be sure of no one knowing, no interruption, playing on his need for confidentiality. And then, she'd received a phone call and had, at the last minute instead suggested his place. He'd been easy to manipulate. Whatever the reason for the last minute change of heart, she'd failed in her mission and that was the real reason she'd left him. She knew that she would be an enemy to both him, and the Russians—the people for whom she was working.

But there was a niggling doubt at the back of his mind. Why had she come back with him to the palace that first night, when she knew she hadn't succeeded? She must surely have been aware of the consequences of failing a mission as delicate as this. A spy would normally have made some excuse and then drifted away into the night. She'd had plenty of opportunities to do just that, but she hadn't. She'd stayed with him for a further three months. Spy or not, their connection had been real. She'd wanted him, as much as he'd wanted her. But desire didn't trump trust. She'd tricked him, she'd taken him for a fool and *that* he would never forgive.

"What would you like me to do?"

Zeeshan's attention snapped back to the investigator on the computer screen in front of him. "Nothing. There's nothing for you to do. I'll sort it out."

"She's with you?"

Zeeshan nodded. "Yes." He sat back heavily in his chair. "She is. Which is strange, is it not?"

He man shrugged. "Maybe better you than the Russians. One of her close friends, a known Russian spy"—he checked some papers—"going by the name of Kirill, was executed shortly before Samantha Cross went missing. She knows what awaits her if they get hold of her. They'll show her no mercy. Whereas you..." He trailed off, unwilling to state the obvious.

"Whereas I *will* show mercy." He looked at the PI bleakly. "And I will continue to do that because that is who I am, and it is exactly that which makes me so objectionable to the Russians. I block their path with my humanity, I stop them from buying power in our countries."

"Yeah," sighed the PI. "You're enemy number one as far as they're concerned, which is out of my league. But I thought you'd be interested in what I'd found out about the girl."

Zeeshan nodded. "I am, thank you. She is with me in the castle now and can't escape, even if she tried."

The PI nodded. "It's always good to have your enemies close."

"Indeed," said Zeeshan. Your friends close, and your enemies closer—he repeated the old adage to himself. But he couldn't help thinking that, in this case, they were one and the same thing.

Zeeshan wasted no more time on the call. There was nothing further he needed to know, nothing more his informant could tell him. There was only person who could tell him everything.

Zeeshan swept out of his office and through the other offices, ignoring everyone including a call from his prime vizier. They could all wait. He continued on to his private quarters, the blood pounding in his ears. He focused on his breathing, willing the raging fire in his veins to fade. It helped, slightly. But he doubted if there were time enough in the world for him to cool his emotions.

He stopped outside her room, his hand on the door, and imagined the scene ahead. But he couldn't. He burst into the room, looking everywhere, but she wasn't there. His tension heightened a notch.

Then he heard some laughter. It was coming from the garden. He glanced briefly down to see her, sitting with a maid, laughing at the antics of a kitten. How could she have done such a thing? Accepted such a task, carried it out despite the fact she'd failed, and then disappeared? And then, here she was, sitting here as if she belonged. She *didn't* belong. There was no room for a traitor in his life.

He left her room and went straight to the garden, stepping out into the sunshine. Both Samantha and the maid looked up, and when the maid saw his face she made her excuses and hurried away. Behind Samantha, showers of water came from the central point of the fountain. Somehow she'd managed to alter the controls so that the water gushed in a torrent, creating small waves on the usually peaceful pond. It seemed fitting. The effect she had on everything around her was always less than peaceful.

"What is it?" she asked. "I don't usually see you at this time. I've just been trying to imagine myself by the sea, with the waves. I can't bear being away from the water for so long." Her smile faded as he approached her, as she sensed his mood was far from peaceful.

She frowned and shook her head. "What on earth has happened?" She reached out to him but he didn't take her hand. Instead, he stopped short and stared at her. How could he have been so stupid, so easily duped by a beautiful woman with a wild heart, to have forgotten all the security measures he usually had in place? All the warnings of the dire consequences of allowing himself to lower his guard and let a woman into his heart?

"I think you know exactly what happened. I only know a part of what happened."

A look of guilt stole across her face. "I don't know what you're talking about."

"I'm talking about how you were paid to seduce me by Russian Intelligence."

What he hadn't been prepared for was the look of pain which entered her eyes. She pushed her hair back from her face and shook her head. "I'm sorry, Zeeshan, I'm so sorry."

He curled his lip into a sardonic smile. "Sorry you've been discovered, but not sorry that you made money from your seduction."

She looked at him and shook her head. "Money?" She held out her empty hands. "Money? Do you see me with any money?"

It was true. He'd collected her from the poorest part of LA, and she had nothing in her apartment, nothing in her suitcase, which he'd made sure was searched on arrival. And the PI hadn't discovered any bank accounts with money stashed away.

"No. But you agreed to seduce me for it. You cannot deny that."

"I don't."

He shrugged. "What you did with the money isn't of any consequence."

"Not even if I told you I gave it away to charity?"

He frowned. "That doesn't make any sense."

"It only makes sense if you regret something you've done, if you're ashamed of it. And, believe me, Zeeshan, I was."

But his anger roiled inside him still, and wouldn't be so easily assuaged.

"Oh, I'm to believe you now, am I? You say you regret seducing me for money, and what? I'm supposed to thank you, and simply kiss and make up." He threw his hands in the air. "It doesn't work like that."

"Then tell me how it works and I'll do whatever it takes."

He huffed a frustrated grunt, took a few steps away and turned his back on her, as he tried to contain the anger and frustration and deep sadness which filled him. It wouldn't do to allow himself to be ruled by this anger. He remembered his father whose every word and every action was governed by anger. He refused to be like him. He wanted to protect his loved ones, not hurt them.

Loved ones, he repeated to himself, closing his eyes, forcing himself to focus on these words. He loved Samantha with all his heart and nothing changed that, not even knowing that she'd betrayed him, tricked him, taken him for a fool. If he was a fool, then so be it. He was a fool who needed to understand what had happened, so he could rectify things and look after his family. He took a deep, calming breath and turned to face her once more.

Samantha had risen from her seat and stood closer to him. She looked pale and drawn and he suddenly realized how much this was all costing her.

"You must tell me everything, Samantha. You know I love you, despite everything. But my love has limits and that limit is lies. I've had enough lies and deceit growing up to last me a lifetime. Tell me everything and then we can figure out where to go from here. And I mean everything," he said, lowering his brow. He had to make her see that this was their last chance at a life together. "No more lies."

She nodded. "It happened on a beach in LA. I was surfing, it had been fantastic, and then afterwards, I went partying with my friends." She shrugged, looking uncomfortable. "I'm not your innocent, naive girl, you know that Zeeshan. I've always liked to party, to drink, to make love to people I wanted to."

He snatched in a breath as she said the last words. "Go on."

"I was approached by a gorgeous-looking surfer who starting telling me about the surf beaches around the world. And then he went on to some more obscure places, places where few people went and yet the surf could be good. Like Ahmar... like Sochi."

"Sochi? In Russia?"

She bit her lip and nodded. "Russia," she confirmed. "The surfer, the man who I became close to, was Russian." She sucked in some air as if willing herself to continue. "I didn't have any money and it turned out Kirill was generous with his, and before I knew it we were traveling the world together."

"You were lovers." The words emerged, not as a question, but as a statement which killed his heart.

"At first, but by the time we came to Ahmar we were just friends. He dared me to try to gain access to your party and to flirt with you. He slipped me a wad of money just for doing that. How much it was, I didn't realize until much later. They were to pay me more after I persuaded you to go to the port building with me. It sounded silly, frivolous fun and that was all that I was in to then. So I agreed."

"And yet you came with me to the palace, instead. Why?"

"Because I wanted to. Because I no longer had any interest in the dare when I was with you."

He shook his head. "And did you truly not consider why he wanted me at the port? Didn't you think, for one minute, how strange that was?"

She grimaced and glanced down. "No. I was naive. I thought it was just a dare. I mean, to seduce a good-looking man at a party was a bit of fun and then to get him outside alone, was…" She lowered her eyes in shame as she realized how innocent she'd been. She took a deep breath, no doubt for courage, and looked him in the eye. "To get you away from the hotel, to the port, alone, would be proof that I'd won the bet."

"And that is all?"

"I swear it. You can trust me."

He shook his head, his lip curling with disgust. Trust. There was that word again. Could he trust her when she'd betrayed him, when her actions were shrouded in mystery and intrigue?

"It doesn't work like that, Samantha. Simply because you wish it, it doesn't come into being. The last thing I can do is trust you." And it bit deep in his heart that he'd revealed the things most secret to the woman it now seemed he could trust the least in the world. He'd have to live with that knowledge, and he'd have to manage that knowledge.

She gripped the folds of his robes, and tears sprang to her eyes. "Zeeshan, please, you must believe me. I heard nothing from him, or any of our other friends, until months later when I was told that he'd been shot dead in the streets of Cairo, assassin style. I was told by the man who'd killed him, someone he'd introduced me to in Russia. This man told me what they wanted me to do."

"Which was?"

"As before, get you alone, get you vulnerable, take you to somewhere where they could capture you."

"And what did you do?"

"What did you think I did? There was no way I was going to betray you then! I'd fallen for you big time. You know I had. You know we were planning a future together. And, at first I thought they'd leave me alone. But they didn't. And then I discovered I was pregnant and I knew my options had narrowed to one. I had to leave."

"You should have told me."

"And risked you rejecting me, but taking our child? I knew how you hated people who betrayed your trust, and I knew how much family meant. I couldn't risk you taking my baby away from me. No, I had to go into hiding—away from you, and away from them. Because they knew where I was, and I knew they would try to use me to get to you."

"And you hid well, until you made the mistake of consulting a doctor."

She bit her lip and nodded. "I made another mistake. I trusted him."

"And it was from that contact that both the Russians and I found you, and discovered you were pregnant." He huffed a grim laugh. "That must have seemed like a prize indeed to them! Another way to get to me."

"Yes, I may have been stupid once, but I worked that one out when my new neighbors told me that people had come looking for me, asking questions, questions that told me it was them. So I moved on and kept moving."

"You should have stayed with me. I could have protected you."

"Really? You *really* would have believed me?" She shook her head wearily. "Zeeshan, you know you wouldn't. And I don't blame you. Nothing in my life up to that point could inspire trust. Nothing."

Zeeshan had no reply. Because she was right. Three months earlier he wouldn't have trusted her. But now? He didn't know.

"So what now?" she asked. He could hear a quaver in her voice, something he'd never heard before. She was never uncertain. And for once in his life, so was he.

"I don't know, Samantha. I truly don't know."

He turned away, but she tightened her grip on his arm. "Zeeshan, don't walk away, please. If you walk away now I'll have lost you, we'll have lost each other, and they will have won."

He turned his head. "They? Samantha, who is they? You could be still be a part of their organization for all I know. How can I trust you?"

"How can you not?"

He turned away from her once more, acutely aware of the feel of her hand still gripping the cloth of his robes, aware of her fragrance and her eyes boring into his back, willing him to believe her. He turned slowly to her, and took her hand and pulled it from him, dropping it by her side. She looked up at him with defeated tears in her eyes. It nearly broke him. Nearly, but not quite.

"Because I don't have to. Because nothing you say makes sense. Because you haven't given me any reason for me to trust you."

He walked away then, closed the door behind him and kept on walking, wishing he could rid himself of her presence in his mind and heart as easily.

CHAPTER 9

*T*ime stood still for Samantha. She couldn't believe that he could walk away from her after all they'd meant to each other. She watched the door slam as a breeze helped it on its way. Even nature was conspiring against her. But what had she expected?

She sat down heavily and put her head in her hands. What she'd expected was an impossible scenario of reconciliation and understanding. Instead, he'd walked away as if it were over. They were over, finished.

She looked at the door through which he'd just walked. She could follow him. She started to rise, but sat back on the stone edging of the fountain. It wouldn't work. She'd told him everything she could and it was up to him now to make up his mind. Did he want her? Or did he want to let her go? The one thing she knew for sure was that she didn't want to be kept in the palace simply because of their child.

He didn't want her because he couldn't trust her. It was that simple, and that difficult. The key was trust but how could she prove to him that he could trust her? She hadn't a clue. The only other thing she had was her love for him, her understanding of him and her respect for him. But would that be enough? She couldn't do anything further, it had to come from him. And all she could do was give him time and hope he'd change his mind.

She walked over to where he'd disappeared, took a deep breath and closed her eyes, imagining she was back in New Zealand, the place of her birth, where she'd been brought up to value freedom. She gripped a trellis, her fingers intertwining with a climbing rose, its thorns digging into her skin. She didn't notice until she saw a trickle of blood running down her hand. But she didn't move. She wanted to feel the pain because, in some peculiar way, it blocked out the pain in her heart. And that was a pain she couldn't do anything about, not until Zeeshan found it in *his* heart to trust her again.

THE NEXT DAY Zeeshan had organized their return to the city. He could keep her as safe in the city as in the desert. Part of his reason to take her to the desert castle had been to be alone with her and to find out her secrets. That he'd done, and he couldn't unknow them, no matter how much he might wish it.

They'd arrived by separate cars and Zeeshan had gone directly to his office. He'd hoped to find it empty but he was surprised to find Adam had made an unexpected visit.

Adam was sitting out on the terrace, his feet on the table, a drink in hand, as he spoke to someone on the computer. Zeeshan shook his head. How anyone could go through life in such a charmed manner as Adam, he had no idea. Even as a youth his youngest brother had escaped much of the drama which had surrounded his family, emerging unscathed. Everyone fell in love with him. Every man wanted him to be his brother or drinking buddy, and every woman wanted him in her bed. Or so Adam would have him believe. And he had no reason to doubt him.

Adam finished the call and greeted Zeeshan. "What's up?" He swung his legs off the table and thrust his hands in his pocket, and stared at Zeeshan. Adam's mother had been French and much adored by his father, and Adam had inherited his mother's beauty and his father's strength. The total package was stunning. And Adam knew it. "You don't look so pleased to see me."

Zeeshan grunted. "It's not all about you, you know. There are other things in this world which make me happy... or not."

Adam smiled, took another sip of his drink and walked over to his desk, while Zeeshan shuffled through some papers.

"Other than me? You wound me, brother."

Zeeshan contented himself with a glare, although it only made Adam's smile broaden. Zeeshan scowled as he returned to trying to find some papers.

"I know what's different about you, apart from that grim face," said Adam.

Zeeshan shot Adam another grim-faced look.

"You're in love!" Adam pointed a finger at Zeeshan. Only his brothers would dare do such a thing. "That's what's different. You're in love with the lovely, blossoming Samantha and you're suffering because of it."

Zeeshan dropped a pile of papers onto the desk. Some of them floated to the floor, disregarded.

Adam noted the untidy papers, and pointed to the mess. "Proves my point."

"This is not some game, Adam."

"Is it not?" asked Adam with irritating levity.

"No, it isn't!" bellowed Zeeshan. "For God's sake, Adam! Be serious for once!"

"Not if I don't have to be. I'll leave 'serious' to you and Rayan. You both do it so much better than me." He finished his drink while Zeeshan stood watching him, infuriated. Adam walked up to him and fingered the papers on his desk. "What is it you're looking for anyway?"

"The prenuptial agreement."

Adam raised an eyebrow. "With the lovely Samantha?"

"Who else?" growled Zeeshan.

Adam glanced down at the papers and plucked out a file. "This looks to be it."

Zeeshan tried to take it from him, but Adam held on to it, took it away from Zeeshan and walked across the room with it, flicking through the pages with an infuriating quickness of eye which belied his laconic manner. Adam, Zeeshan knew, was far cleverer, far sharper, than he admitted to being. "This looks straightforward."

"And what makes you the expert? Ah, that's right," he said facetiously. "Your law degree. Although how you managed to pass your examinations, when you spent your years at Harvard chasing as many women as you could, defeats me."

Adam glanced up from the papers with a grin. "You got that wrong. I didn't have to do much chasing. Anyway, it defeated my professors, too." Adam tossed the papers back on the desk. "Suffice to say I am far cleverer than I look."

"Yes, and I know that to my cost."

Adam's smile slipped from his face and he frowned in concentration. "Seriously, Zeeshan, what do you want to do with it? It looks pretty standard to me."

"Why would I tell you anything?"

"Because I'm the only person you can talk to? Rayan is too embroiled with his family, and you are hardly going to confide in your staff. That's not you."

Zeeshan felt the force of anger leave him like the wind

leaving sails. He sat down, feeling suddenly exhausted and defeated.

"You're right. You're the only person I can tell."

"The only person without a life." Zeeshan shot him a hard look. "Okay, okay. I know, it's not only about me. This time, anyway. Shoot. Tell me what's given my honorable, self-disciplined brother such a raging mood."

"It's Samantha."

Adam folded his arms and leant back against the desk. "I know that much. What's she done to make you so angry?"

Zeeshan said the words which had been repeating in his mind like a damning mantra. "She betrayed me."

"Betrayal," said Adam, in a different kind of voice. "Ah, now you are definitely talking serious. You would forgive many things, but not betrayal. What did she do?"

"She was working for the Russians. It was for them that she seduced me."

Zeeshan had never heard such swear words uttered by any of his family before. For a moment he wondered where on earth Adam had learned them, but then he reckoned his youngest brother had led a far more interesting life than he had.

"She's working for the Russians?" Adam pushed his fingers through his hair and twisted one way and then the other as he processed this fact. "So have you sent her away?"

"Of course not, Adam. You've forgotten one thing—she's pregnant with my child."

"Are you sure it's your child?"

Zeeshan felt an immediate blast of anger that Adam could think such a thing of Samantha but realized it was illogical. Hadn't he wondered the same thing? "Yes, I am. The doctor in LA confirmed it. And I'm not about to let a child of mine live away from me. You, of all people, must understand that."

Adam's usually smiling mouth was a grim line and he

gave a brief nod. A whole world of suffering and pain lay behind it. One of the things that bound the three brothers so tightly together.

"You must keep them both here, with you. Of course you must. But is there a chance that she was somehow tricked into this? I mean, why would they be searching for her, hunting her down in the States, if she was working for them?"

It had been something which had been preying on Zeeshan's mind. There could be only one answer.

"Because she'd changed her mind."

"A woman's prerogative," suggested Adam.

"Not this woman. Samantha's mind is always made up about everything."

Adam shrugged. "Then perhaps she didn't realize what she was getting into? Perhaps they recruited her through a second party to use her without her knowledge?"

Zeeshan pursed his lips as he considered the matter.

"Come on, Zeeshan, it's the most likely thing that could have happened. Maybe she simply thought flirting with you might have been fun. Of course, she didn't know you weren't the flirtatious sort. Now, if *I'd* been there..." He trailed off after he registered Zeeshan's dirty look. Adam laughed and held up his hand. "Come on, Zeeshan. Put your macho pride aside and think about it for a minute. You only have to look at her, be in her company for a few minutes, to realize that she's exactly the sort of woman the Russians would recruit—someone who was vulnerable and hadn't a clue that they were being manipulated. There's a charming naiveté about her."

"Who knows? Maybe, maybe not."

"You'll have to give her the benefit of the doubt. You've no choice. After all, you'll be a father to her child." Adam stood up, and swiped up his phone from the coffee table. "Anyway I must be off. It's up to you. You can either keep your child and the woman you love—"

"I don't—" Adam held up his hand and ignored Zeeshan's interruption.

"Or you can reject them both, and then where will you be?"

Zeeshan felt tortured and torn. "She betrayed me, Adam. She did what my enemies wanted her to do."

"But not for the same reason. I'd lay my life on it. They wanted you separated from your people, vulnerable, so they could get to you, and they used Samantha to do that. Samantha was in it for the fun. And, when she discovered that she'd stepped into hot water, and was likely to put you in even hotter water, she changed the plan." He leaned forward, emphasizing the words. "She changed the plan, changed her mind. That much is obvious."

"To you, maybe."

"Think about it, Zeeshan. Vent your macho anger, deal with your humiliation and think about it. Because your future depends upon it."

Zeeshan forgot his own troubles for a moment and stared at his brother. When had Adam gotten so wise? For a few moments Adam held his gaze and Zeeshan looked, really looked, into those eyes, and knew he'd been missing something. Something was troubling his youngest brother whose heart he'd thought was Teflon-coated.

He opened his mouth to speak but Adam, obviously sensing something of what had passed through Zeeshan's mind, raised his hand in warning and shook his head.

"Don't," said Adam.

And Zeeshan didn't. He closed his mouth and watched Adam leave the room without a further exchange of words.

He shook his head and looked away. He had enough on his plate without trying to figure out what was wrong with

Adam. That would have to wait another day. But what he would do was take on board Adam's advice, because he knew, deep down, that it was good.

But there was no doubt Adam was way off the mark when it came to Zeeshan's version of self-reflection. Whereas Rayan would escape on his horse into the desert, and Adam would go somewhere where the nightlife and people could absorb his pent-up energy, Zeeshan had no intention of doing any of these things. He had only one place he knew which would give him the peace to think things through properly.

SAMANTHA RUSHED to the door at the sound of a sharp rap. She flung the door open wide, hardly daring to hope that Zeeshan would have forgiven her, but simply relieved that he'd returned to her. But it wasn't Zeeshan standing there. Instead, Adam stood, his hands thrust in the pockets of his trousers, looking as if he were making a casual call. She felt her face drop, and her disappointment must have been plain to see, because Adam's lips curled into a smile.

"Even though it's obvious it's not me you wish to see, I wonder if you could spare me a few moments?"

She summoned up a ghost of a smile. "Sure." She stepped to one side. "Come in."

She followed him inside, her mind racing as to what he could possibly want with her. It didn't take long to find out. Still with his back to her, he picked up a photo from the sideboard. He gazed at it intently for a few moments before turning to her. He held out the photo for her to see.

Puzzled, she took the photo and looked at it. It showed Zeeshan and his father and mother and no other siblings.

"A family photo," said Adam wryly.

"But it's only of him. Where were the rest of you?"

"Good question." He took the photo back from her and placed it on the shelf. "The answer to which lies at the heart of all this mess."

He turned to face her and she felt uncertain under his laser-sharp gaze. She suspected that nothing got past Adam and his sharp intellect, not even the women he seduced. She thought he probably understood everything perfectly.

"I'm sorry, I don't understand."

"I'm not surprised. No doubt your own family is a whole lot simpler than ours."

She raised an eyebrow and sighed. "We were certainly fewer in number, but the issues"—she shrugged—"the issues were still there."

He grinned and she couldn't help returning his grin. "You know, I didn't realize you were like this. We should have met sooner. It would make things easier."

"For whom?"

He glanced at her again. "For my brother, Zeeshan, of course. I would have helped you to understand him because, knowing him, he's unlikely to give you any assistance."

"Ah." She nodded. "That would be wonderful. I need all the help I can get." She smiled uncertainly while he was silent. "I'm sorry, would you care for a drink?"

He shook his head. "No, thank you. I'm here for a few minutes only. I'm meeting someone. She'll be cursing me for my tardiness already. I'm here because I want you to know that Zeeshan's life has been built around trust. That is, knowing *who* he can trust and *who* he can't. Without those antennae he feels lost. And you've made him feel lost because his antennae failed him with you."

"I know. It really isn't as it seems, you know. I was a fool, chasing passing pleasures, accepting people at face value. I wish I'd had the smallest part of Zeeshan's antennae to see me through, but I didn't. And I trusted people I shouldn't have. But, you must believe me, as soon as I discovered I was being used to get to Zeeshan, I distanced myself from my old friends."

"And you saved Zeeshan's life by doing that."

"Yes, and I endangered mine, which was why I had to leave. Can you help me convince Zeeshan that I speak the truth?"

"No, I can't. That's down to you."

"I've tried to contact him but he's not answering my calls and I've been blocked from going to his offices."

"Maybe you're looking in the wrong places."

"Is he in the palace?"

"Yes. I know exactly where he'll be. Where he's always gone for solace. To his books. To the old library. That was his place. And, I'm sure, still is. Go there, and give him time to understand. He's taken it hard but I'm sure you'll be able to convince him." His smile split into a warm grin. "After all, you've convinced me, and I'm much harder to convince." His phone buzzed once more. "Right, I must go. And so must you. Go find your lover and heal the differences between you. I'm sure you'll be all the stronger for it."

"I hope so. Thank you for coming."

"My pleasure." He appeared undecided, and then nodded to her and walked out the door without a further word. Samantha watched him go with a smile. She imagined Adam was usually far more demonstrative with women but wasn't accustomed to interacting with his brother's pregnant lover, and had decided a distant approach was required. At least she had an ally in Adam.

His visit had changed her anxiety to determination. She understood Zeeshan a little more and, even better, she now knew where to find him.

. . .

THE ANCIENT LIBRARY with its dusty, papery smells had welcomed Zeeshan like an old friend. And not just any old friend, but a friend who wouldn't double-cross, a friend who could always be trusted to offer wisdom and comfort— things he couldn't get from anyone else.

The library was in the oldest part of the building, and its lofty pillars supported a decorated ceiling of rare beauty. The walls were lined with book shelves which held some of the most precious books on Ahmari culture and history. Modern precautions had been installed unobtrusively to ensure their safety. But it left the library intact, with an air of silence and antiquity which never failed to settle Zeeshan.

Initially he'd trailed his fingers along the bumpy backs of the books, feeling the soft leather and the gilded letters, allowing them to soothe his soul. Then he searched for a specific volume. He carefully laid it out on the table, beautifully inlaid with different woods and polished until it shone. Slowly he turned the delicate pages until he found the page he was looking for. It was about forgiveness—something which came naturally to him, but less so to his fellow men, especially his brothers. He needed a reminder that it was okay to do what his heart wanted.

"It is a mercy from Allah that you were gentle with them. If you had been rough or hard of heart, they would have scattered from around you. So pardon them and ask forgiveness for them."

He'd entered the library knowing what he'd wanted to do. But he'd needed confirmation. And here it was in the *Surah Al 'Imran* of the Quran, exactly as he remembered it. He walked around the table and sat at the desk, thinking about the words, thinking about Adam's words, and, most of all, thinking about the woman who had shaken up his world so dramatically.

He didn't know how many hours had passed, but the sun

had lowered and its rich rays shone through the shuttered windows, highlighting dust motes. It was as if he'd been half-asleep, or in a reverie, because suddenly he was startled by a sound. He looked over and saw the door handle move. Who dared enter this place without so much as a knock?

He strode over to the door and pulled it open.

Samantha was wearing the most brilliant of gauzy robes, the color of the setting sun. Her blonde hair formed a halo around her face. For a moment he thought he was seeing things. Then she smiled, a tentative smile which was at odds with her confident dress and hair. She stepped forward and reached out to him.

"Zeeshan?" she said, in a soft, husky voice, with the upward intonation of a question. The combination of her brilliant appearance, her vulnerability and her insecurity got to him.

He caught her hand in his and tugged her gently towards him, searching her face, still trying to convince himself that she wasn't a figment of his imagination.

"Samantha!"

"I'm so sorry. I've never knowingly betrayed you, and never will." Tears glazed her eyes as she pleaded with him to believe her.

He was speechless as he fell into the pools of her eyes, unable to imagine how he could possibly have thought that she could have betrayed him. He could feel the truth of her words in every part of him. She *was* a part of him now. And he knew she felt the same. She could no more have betrayed him, than have betrayed herself. Their futures were bound together.

A tear trickled down her cheek and her lips quivered as she opened her mouth. "Please, Zeeshan, you must forgive me." Her voice broke as she gasped in a lungful of air, trying desperately to control her feelings. She clutched at his robes like a dying woman. "I can't bear that you believe I would harm you. Believe me, as soon as I discovered how I was being used I walked away, not wanting to be a part of it. What I hadn't realized was that I'd become a part of it, whether I liked it, or not."

He pulled her close, unable to bear the vulnerability he could see in her eyes. She pressed her cheek to his chest and he kissed the top of her head.

"Tell me that you forgive me, Zeeshan, please," she said, her voice muffled against his chest and robes.

He held her away from him and shook his head. The tears multiplied down her face.

"No. But I'll show you."

CHAPTER 10

Zeeshan tilted up her chin, and without wiping away her tears, pressed his lips to hers. The salt from her tears combined with her lipstick and the faint trace of mint that lingered on her tongue as he slid his along hers. They went from zero to a hundred in seconds. Suddenly their need was intense and he pulled her into the room and banged the door closed against the world.

Their kisses became more intense and she pressed her body to his, her swollen stomach creating a distance he didn't want. And, nor, it seemed did she.

She turned around in his arms and he put his hands over her breasts, flicking his fingers over her nipples, loving the sound of her moan with pleasure. He nuzzled her neck as he lifted the diaphanous layers of her dress, tugging it up until he felt her bare thighs. He breathed her in, as he slid his hands down her trembling thighs and then higher until he found what he was seeking.

He grunted with approval as he found no underwear to impede him, only a slickly-wet, needy sex which his fingers wasted no time in exploring. Giving pleasure to the woman who meant more to him than anyone else in the world—more to him than any notion of honor or trust or forgiveness—was all he wanted. At least for now.

She fell back against him as he supported her with one hand and pleasured her with his other hand. It took only seconds for her breathing to hitch and for her gasps to turn to cries of release. And he knew that she'd got a whole lot more than simple pleasure. He'd given her the answer she wanted—forgiveness. And he'd given her the relief she wanted from her pain and sadness.

She twisted her head and their lips met once more but only in a brief kiss this time. He was too hard for her, his need to great. But he wanted her naked first.

He fumbled with the fastenings of her dress. She gave a low laugh as she turned to face him. She stepped away, released the dress and stood naked before him. She looked magnificent. Her breasts had always been full, but they were even larger now. And with her pregnant stomach, she looked the epitome of sexual femininity.

It was his turn for the tears to spring to his eyes.

She frowned. "Are you crying?"

He shook his head resolutely. "Of course not," he said, willing the tears to disappear, but they didn't. "It's you. You are so beautiful, you make my eyes water, as if I'm looking directly at the sun."

Her frown changed to a seductive smile. "Then close your eyes."

He did as she'd suggested. He thought he'd do anything for her at that moment. He sucked in a harsh gasp as he felt her hands on his bone-hard cock which she'd released from his clothes. She held him within her hands but he wanted more.

He opened his eyes and, after kissing her, turned her in his arms. He bent her over the back of a chaise longue and she lay her head on her folded arms for all the world as if she were about to have a nap. But she raised her bottom toward him and he needed no further invitation.

He thrust himself slowly into her, hardly drawing breath as he felt her tight, moist heat around him. For a moment he felt weakened by the extreme pleasure which flowed into every part of his body. But when he entered her fully with a quick thrust, she gave such an orgasmic cry that all thought of weakness fled. He was in control of her every feeling, thought and emotion and he would make sure she knew it.

He held tight onto her hips, making sure he had full control as he thrust into her. He looked straight out to the distant mountains which were framed in the window over her head. He continued to thrust, feeling white-hot, his eyes blinded by the light, and by the passion which surged inside him. Nothing could make him whole again except this.

Suddenly the world around him collapsed and focused on this one point, this one connection—physical, mental and spiritual—he had with this woman. He came inside of her at the same time as her muscles spasmed around him, drawing as much of him as she could inside of her.

Their breathing slowed and he withdrew. He held her close to him, turning her around until she was snuggled into his side. He smoothed his hands around her body.

"Is it truly all right between us, Zeeshan?"

"Yes, Sammie. It always was, and it always will be. There's nothing that can change that. We're meant to be together, and be together we will be."

It was only after they were both dressed he remembered the meeting he had to attend.

He helped her fasten her clothes and kissed her tenderly. "I must go, now, Samantha. I have business to attend to."

"Anything I should know about?"

He hesitated. Should he tell her about the threat from the

Russians? He couldn't bear that look of vulnerability and fear returning. He shook his head. "Nothing I can't deal with. Rest, explore the palace, go where you will. You're free to do whatever you choose. Just don't wander far."

"I thought you said I was safe?"

"You are. I just want to make sure you *remain* safe." He kissed her. "I have to go now."

They walked hand in hand out of the library and back to the newer wing of the palace. With another quick kiss, he'd passed through to the public offices. He glanced back once and smiled at her. She blew a kiss and he didn't think he'd ever felt so happy, knowing she'd be there when he returned.

"Zeeshan!" He heard her call, but his attention was taken up with other people. He saw her lips move but couldn't hear her question. He smiled and waved his hand, acceding to whatever question she asked. He'd give her the world if he could.

SAMANTHA PRACTICALLY FLOATED BACK to her rooms. That he'd given her permission to go wherever she wanted to, within or outside the palace—she'd taken his wave as answering her question in the affirmative—had lightened her spirit. And she knew exactly where she was going to go. It would be safe. From one corner of the palace, the sea was only a few hundred meters away. And she couldn't wait.

She picked out a full burkha from her wardrobe—something which would enable her to fit in to the outside world and not be identified—and headed for the shower.

ZEESHAN HADN'T EVER SEEN his advisors looks so grim. Rayan had joined Adam, who looked up at him with a grin. Zeeshan looked away quickly. His younger brother was far too observant.

Zeeshan sat at the head of the table. "So what's the urgency? What's happened?"

"It's the Russians," said Rayan. "Our sources say that their plans are intensifying. They're still determined to destabilize the region."

"What are they planning?"

"Our sources say that they'll try anything, but their first plan is the least expensive, and most explosive."

Zeeshan knew what Rayan was about to say, he could feel the horror in the pit of his stomach. "To kill me."

Rayan gave one short sharp nod.

"They're awaiting their chance, Zeeshan. You have to be extremely careful from now on," said Adam.

"I'm always careful. There's no way they can get to me. I'm quite safe. Don't worry about me. Worry about yourself and your family."

"I don't have to. The Russians don't want us. They want only one person — you."

"I've told you. There's no way they can get to me."

"Intelligence says that they believe they have a way."

"How?" scoffed Zeeshan.

"The word appears to be Russian for 'weakness'. But I don't think they know you very well. They don't know you don't have a weakness," said Rayan with a wry smile.

Zeeshan frowned and jumped up. Rayan might not believe he had a weakness, but he knew he had. Only one. But she was safe, hidden away like a special jewel, deep within the palace. Nothing could touch her. She was safe, he repeated, as he paced up and down the room.

"Zeeshan! What is it? Is there something we don't know about?" asked Rayan

He stopped pacing and faced his brothers. He gritted his teeth as he tried to find it within him to tell them the truth.

"Zeeshan?" asked Rayan, the more serious of his two younger brothers. "What is it? Tell me."

"Zeeshan has only one weakness. Samantha," said Adam. "Am I right?"

Zeeshan gave a quick nod.

Rayan came and placed his hand on Zeeshan's shoulder. "It's okay. I understand about love, now. She might be your weakness, but know this, Zeeshan. She will also be your strength."

Adam rolled his eyes.

Despite himself, Zeeshan smiled. "You've become wise in your old age, brother."

Rayan didn't return the smile. "You'd better believe it." He squeezed Zeeshan's shoulder. "Now, if the Russians really do believe your weakness is Samantha, you'd best go to her, warn her. It seems they'll likely do anything to draw her out. And if they get hold of her?" He shrugged. "They've got hold of you, too."

Zeeshan shook his head. "She won't go. There's nothing they could tempt her with."

"Who said anything about tempting? They'll stop at nothing to get to you."

He grimaced and gave a quick nod. "I'll go and update her." He imagined her turning to him with that heart-stopping look of surprise when he appeared earlier than expected. He then imagined the course of events things would take. "I think work's over for one day."

He grinned at his brothers. "I'll see you tomorrow for the betrothal ceremony. Who have you brought, Adam?"

Adam looked strangely uncomfortable. "You'll see tomorrow."

Zeeshan wasted no further time in talking to his brothers and quickly went in search of Samantha.

SAMANTHA LOVED THE PALACE, loved the grounds, loved everything about this new land she'd found herself in, and she particularly loved the fresh air of freedom which she gulped into her lungs as she hurried away from the palace grounds.

She could barely stop herself from grinning like a mischievous child as she remembered the mistake the guard had made by opening a set of doors which was normally barred to her. For her own safety, Zeeshan reckoned, but how risky could it be to go walking within minutes from the palace?

Not risky at all, Samantha reassured herself, looking around at the smart buildings which surrounded the palace. But it wasn't those which lured her on. She gulped down a lungful of fresh, salty air and pictured the sea, which she could smell as it was so very close, and which she hadn't visited since her return. It had only been a short time, but she felt as if every pore in her body needed air, sunshine, the wind in her hair and the waves around her feet. Especially the waves around her feet.

She looked around greedily and did a double-take at a glint of sunlight which shone in her eyes from a nearby roof. She looked again, but there was nothing. She must have been imagining things.

She walked quickly from the rear palace gates skirting the bustling old city, confident that her full burkha would disguise her identity, even if there were any danger, and she was confident there couldn't be.

Despite the lateness of the hour, she was beginning to feel dizzy and queasy under her dark burkha. In her haste to get away, she'd over-estimated her ability to deal with the heat, which was more intense in the city. She glanced back. The palace was reassuringly close. She could even see the shadowy figures of people inside. She'd only be gone a few minutes. She quickly crossed the road to the quayside.

It was a relief to breathe in the cooler air there. But there were only boats bobbing alongside the quay. She looked longingly towards the beaches a little distance away. Waves pounded onto the white sand. It was as if she had no say in the matter, and she started walking towards the sandy beach, drawn by the sound of the surf. The smell of the salty sea drifted into the air as the waves hit the rocks which marked the beginning of the beach.

The beach was deserted. She looked around, but there was nobody watching, and she walked down the steps onto the sand. She slipped off her shoes and closed her eyes in relief at the feel of the hot, gritty sand sifting up between her toes. She walked on toward the sea, drawn by the splash of waves upon the sand.

Surely a paddle wouldn't hurt? There was nobody around so she carefully lifted her burkha and stepped into the water. It felt delicious, as if it were feeding her, as if she were drinking in the cool water into her body. As she moved her feet through the water, watching the water ripple and seeing the shells in the sand glinting in the sunlight, she heard the sound of a motor boat approaching. She thought nothing of it as she was so close to the harbor. She only looked up once the boat had drifted a little closer towards her.

There were two men on board, fishermen by their appearance. They didn't come any closer but she knew it was time to go. Before she'd even cleared the water she let her burkha drop and collected her sandals. But when she looked up from picking up her sandals she found two men standing before her. She gasped in surprise. Last time she'd looked there been nobody behind her, and now these heavily-built men were staring at her, their expressions fierce.

She sidestepped them, keeping her head bowed, muttering courtesies in Arabic as she stumbled through the soft sand trying to make her way back to the steps.

Suddenly, there was a shout from the sea and she glanced around. That was her undoing. The boat had come to shore quietly behind her and when she turned around the two men were upon her, clamping a foul smelling cloth to her face. She only had time to struggle briefly before everything turned black.

CHAPTER 11

*Z*eeshan looked at his assistant in disbelief. "What do you mean, she's gone?"

His assistant shot a sideways looks at his other advisers, obviously hoping for some back-up, but none was forthcoming. Instead, his trusted advisers shuffled from foot to foot, looking uncomfortable, and occasionally exchanging glances with each other.

He slammed his fist onto the desk. "Tell me what the hell you mean!"

In the end it was one of the younger men who had the courage to answer.

"Apparently she left wearing a burkha through the servant's gate. The guards didn't realize who she was until it was too late."

Zeeshan looked out the window at the city where she could be wandering at that very moment. She was vulnerable in the extreme, although she might not realize it. He couldn't bear the thought. What the hell had made her do it? He closed his eyes at the memory of their last exchange of words. He'd verbally given her her freedom, with the proviso that she stay within the palace grounds. But she hadn't heard, she couldn't have heard. He gripped the phone on the desk and threw it across the room, needing to vent his rage and frustration physically.

"Get the police! Get the army. Get anyone who can find her!" He glared at the men who surrounded him, stunned into immobility by his shouted command. He never shouted, he'd never had any need to before, but now he did. His heart was screaming for them to find her. "Now!" he bellowed. "Whatever you need," he said impressing his words into their minds. "I want her back *here*, with *me*."

He watched them leave, all but his young assistant.

"We will find her, Your Majesty."

He was like steel—unfeeling, hard and impregnable. He didn't dare feel anything different. He didn't dare *feel*. "Do whatever you have to do, lean on anyone you have to, but find her."

Then he turned and walked swiftly to the door.

"Your Majesty!" called his anxious assistant. He barely heard. But he was aware of the man's grip on his arm, something no one ever did. "Your Majesty!" his assistant repeated. "You cannot go after her."

"How dare you touch me! How dare you speak to me like that! Of course I will go."

"Your Majesty! You cannot. You're needed here. Besides, our intelligence believe *you* to be the target, not Miss Cross."

Zeeshan knew they were correct, but didn't care. There was only one person who was important now, and it wasn't him. It was a woman who he loved more than his own life.

"I'm going to look for my fiancée. Come with me if you must, gather security around me if you must, but know this, there is no way in this world I'm sitting in my palace, waiting for someone to find her."

His robes billowed around him as he walked through the

doors and closed them behind them. Only when he was on his own did he allow the tears of rage, impotence and frustration to fall as he paced the office. How could he have been so stupid as to let her out of his sight? She was a woman accustomed to getting her own way, and needing, at a fundamental level, a sense of freedom which he had robbed her of. Yes, he may have wanted to protect her, but he'd succeeded in doing the reverse, driving her away from him and into danger.

Because Samantha had fallen off the face of the earth, and he knew what that meant. His enemies had taken her. But it wasn't her they wanted, it was him. And he was quite prepared to surrender himself to get her back if necessary.

SAMANTHA SAT on the wooden chair, tied securely, a piece of cloth stuffed into her mouth, which was covered, and tied at the back. She'd arrived in the night and it was still night. That was all she knew. At some point she'd dozed but had awoken just as she and the chair were about to topple. Then she'd given up on sleep, aware that the danger grew as morning approached.

Suddenly a light went on outside, and it shone through the broken masonry of the covered windows. Through the cracks in the concrete ceiling, she could see where she was for the first time. It was worse than she'd imagined, and she hadn't imagined lovely.

The place was filthy, rags stuffed into holes to try to block out the light, the floor littered with dead rodents. She shuddered. She didn't even want to imagine what the scuttling in the dark had been. And worse than any of this was the lack of sound. She couldn't hear anyone talking or moving. She could hear no clank of machinery, nor whirr of a motor to indicate civilization was close by. She could tell by her parched throat that she was far from water. She suspected she'd been drugged and taken into the desert where no one could find her. She didn't know what was worse, being alone, or someone coming for her.

She soon found out. When she heard footsteps approaching from a long way off, she knew that having company would be infinitely worse.

When the door opened and a harsh beam of artificial light streamed into the room, Samantha was momentarily blinded. The man didn't move, and kept the door open. She squinted to try to discern his features but his face was in shadow, haloed by flood lights. All she could tell was that he was slight but held himself like a fighter. His arms were by his side, and she could see quite clearly that his hands were balled into fists.

He didn't speak at first but walked around her, like a lion inspecting his prey, chewing something which smelt strange. At least she could see his face better, could gauge him. The terror which sat in the pit of her stomach increased at the sight of his scarred face and cold, hard gaze. He was assessing her. Then he undid her gag and tossed it aside.

"How much longer do you wish to live?" he asked, with a heavy Russian accent.

She closed her eyes to stop the tears which had immediately sprung into her eyes and tried to flex her hands, but they were bound too tightly. A surge of adrenalin filled her and she opened her eyes again.

"You cannot touch me."

"We already have. And we will do more than touch you if you prove troublesome."

Samantha tried to calm her breathing. She couldn't afford for him to see how frightened she was. She had her baby to think about. "What is it you want from me?"

He stopped pacing and stood in front of her again, but

closer now. He smelled of stale sweat and a peculiar odor she couldn't place.

"What we want is information."

A wave of relief swept over her. At least they wanted something. She had something to bargain for her baby's life. "What kind?"

"The kind of information which relates to your lover— Sheikh Zeeshan ibn Mohammed Aziz, King of Ahmar, to be exact."

She pressed her lips together in alarm and shook her head. "I don't know anything."

He gave a chilling laugh, revealing black teeth, and sat on a corner of a broken wooden pallet. "And I think you do."

She shook her head again, stronger this time. "I know nothing."

"Don't take me for a fool. You fuck him, you must know something."

She shook her head and he caught her chin in a vise-like grip, his fingers digging into her cheeks. "You failed us once, you will not fail us again. Do you know what we do to people who fail us? People who don't do as we wish?"

She shook her head.

He grunted with grim amusement. "You'll find out soon enough. We don't take kindly to people double-crossing us." He released her face with a sharp twist which she felt in the back of her neck. She winced.

"I didn't double-cross you."

"You didn't do as you were told. We told you to take him to the port but you didn't."

"He didn't want to go, and I didn't see there was a problem."

"There was a very big problem and your friend paid the price for it."

Samantha swallowed down the sudden surge of fear.

She'd been right. Kirill had been killed by the men he'd introduced her to when they'd been surfing in Sochi, the same people who were behind the dare for her to lure Zeeshan to the port. And now it was her turn.

She felt his finger trail down her cheek, her neck and stop at the top of her breasts. "But it doesn't have to be like that."

She felt sick and couldn't answer for fear of vomiting.

He smiled and withdrew his hand, and stood in front of her.

"I'll try to make things easy for you to understand. We need information to take Zeeshan down, to depose him. He's a problem for my government and we need him gone. What do you know that we can use?"

That he's not the true king.

The thought popped, unbidden, into her mind. It was the kind of intelligence the man wanted and could make use of. Zeeshan had trusted her with a truth which he'd only told his brothers before. And that truth could buy her her freedom, because it was exactly what this man was looking for. Maybe it was what he suspected. She shook her head vehemently.

"I don't believe you," he sneered. "There's something, isn't there?"

"No, there's nothing. What could there be?"

"I don't know, but I'm going to keep you here to find out what you know. Because I can see from those big blue eyes that you know something useful."

"I know nothing."

"Come on," he said, trailing his finger across her cheek, lingering on her lips, dragging it down until she tasted him. She nearly gagged but couldn't move to protect herself. "A beautiful woman like you. I'm sure when you make love to the king he gives you more than his cock." He moved closer "He gives you secrets. All you need to do is tell me them. That's all. Then you'll be free."

She shook her head.

The man turned a chair around and sat down, his arms around its back, his face close to hers. His jeans strained across his thighs. "Did you enjoy having a man such as he inside you?" He leaned even closer so she could smell his breath—a disgusting smell which reminded her of nail polish remover, and she could see red spittle in the corner of his mouth. She suddenly realized he was chewing betel nut. That would explain the black teeth. He turned and spat bright red spittle onto the floor. Her throat constricted in disgust.

She shook her head, determined not to answer him, not to say anything which could excite him further.

"Whether he took you willingly or not, you didn't take any protection, did you? He planted his seed into you. Or maybe it's not his? Maybe you're a whore who has sex with anyone?"

He jumped up and threw the chair to one side. For a moment she thought he'd walk away, but then he turned and came back to her. He stood, his crotch at her eye level, forcing her to see what he could do to her if he wished it.

"You have a choice before you, Samantha," he said softly. "You can give us information or, I promise you, you and that baby of yours will be hurt." He stepped away and spat again to one side. "Your choice." He walked out of the room and closed the door behind him. The flood light snapped off, leaving her in darkness and with a sense of terror which refused to leave her.

ZEESHAN RECEIVED word from his chief of security in the early hours of the morning. In the interim, he'd scoured the city and port, had talked with both his army and navy and was now in a convoy crossing the desert. It was a guess, but an educated one. They could be nowhere else but lost in the immense emptiness of the desert, which stretched from his to the neighbouring countries. A no-man's-land of emptiness in which people could easily disappear.

He pressed the cellphone to his ear. "Yes?"

"We know where she is."

The intensity of the relief which filled Zeeshan surprised him. He hadn't known he could feel such emotion.

"Tell me."

"She is still here in Ahmar, thanks to the blockade. They tried to get her out across the sea, but had to turn around when they saw our ships. It was there that we detected them. Their boat has been discovered and we believe they headed into the desert. Your drivers are being informed of the co-ordinates at this moment."

Zeeshan's blood chilled. "Who has her?" But even before the answer came, he knew. "It's the Russians, isn't it?"

"Yes."

Zeeshan swore under his breath. He knew it would be, but had hoped it might be some minor kidnapping, her return in exchange for money. But it was far worse. Nobody had yet dealt effectively with the Russians. They wanted more than money.

"She is close to the border," continued his security chief. "They will be biding their time until they can get out. And then—"

"And then it will be too late," said Zeeshan, dully. He discontinued the call as the driver revved the car, driving it faster into the desert. But not fast enough for Zeeshan.

ZEESHAN PUT down the night vision binoculars through which he could make out the heavily guarded semi-derelict buildings. It didn't look like they were aware of their presence—yet.

They were surrounded. There was no chance of anyone escaping, taking Samantha with them, but still... He looked at the soldier who was organizing the rescue with impatience. He, too, had his night vision glasses trained on the cluster of houses before them. There wasn't a sound. He could feel the impatience growing inside of him. If the man didn't act any time soon, he'd do it for him. He felt a growl of impatience and frustration build inside of him.

He couldn't bear to think about what they might be doing to her at that very moment. He closed his eyes tight. Suddenly there was a movement. He opened his eyes to see the man had dropped his hand, and other men were moving forward in a crouched position, silently advancing on the buildings in the pitch darkness. At last.

Zeeshan did as he'd been told—now wasn't the time to make demands, now was the time to listen to his staff who were experts in such things—and he followed in the second line of men. Far ahead in the darkness he heard a volley of gunshots and then nothing.

He pressed his earpiece into his ear so he could hear the leader's commentary more clearly. He followed his chief of operations up to the cluster of houses, towards the rear one. The door was wide open but it was dark.

"She's in here, Your Majesty," he heard through his earpiece. They were having problems. He couldn't bear it any longer.

Ignoring the warnings of his guards, he sprinted up to the front with the others. Gunfire had given way to hand-to-hand combat, and he arrived just in time to place a well-aimed blow on someone about to hit one of his men. With the way clear, he launched himself amid the confusion at the door where everything seemed to be focused. The door was rotten and he burst in upon two men crouching in the corner of the room. With a roar he was upon them, grabbing them both and flinging them across the room, where his men dealt with them. By the time he'd ended up fighting another man who'd sprung upon him from a corner, there were bodies laid out around the room, and the pungent smell of blood mingled with the stale smell of the rat-infested room.

As his breathing heaved, his eyes sought what he was looking for. At first sight the place was empty. He was about to leave, believing his staff had got it wrong, when he heard a whimper coming from the corner. His head jerked and his eyes narrowed as he tried to see into the corner which, he suddenly realized, was darker than the surrounding shadows.

"Samantha?" he rasped. "Is that you?"

She cried out but didn't move. When he moved closer to her, flicking his torch forward, he saw why. She was tied to a chair which had been pushed, or had fallen, to the floor. He knelt at her feet, pushing the hair back from her face, needing to be reassured, but what he saw did nothing to reassure him.

"What have they done to you, Sammie?"

Tears streaked across her face in dusty streams, and she sobbed as others came in and cut her bindings. Carefully he held her in his arms and allowed her to sob for a few seconds before lifting her. The sobbing intensified. He murmured soothing noises in her ear as he carried her outside. He needed to get her away from here as soon as possible, needed to heal her, to make her well, to care for her and never let her go again.

"What did the bastards do to you?"

She gulped. "Zeeshan? Is that really you?" And in that moment he saw the bruise which spread over her temple. She'd been knocked out, which accounted for her dazed appearance.

"Yes, it's me. What have they done to you?" But he didn't wait for an answer, instead he carried her out of the rough hut toward a waiting car. He'd let his staff sort out the rest of them. They knew what to do. He'd deal with his prisoners tomorrow, but tonight he only had one thing on his mind, and that was to bring his beloved back home where she belonged.

He placed her carefully beside him in the front seat of the car and drove off, with security motorbikes leading the way. He should have laid her down on the rear seat, but he couldn't bear for her to be out of his sight. This way, driving with one hand on the wheel, the other on her, he knew she was safe.

"Zeeshan," she whispered. It didn't matter how low her voice, he thought he'd hear her above the loudest noise. He glanced at her, gripped her hand and then gritted his teeth to cope with the rough terrain.

"Don't speak. We'll be at the airbase soon, and then we'll be back at the palace before you know it and you can leave all this behind you."

"No, I have to speak. I'm sorry. I'm so sorry. I'm made a mess of things from day one. My mother was right. I am hopeless, a loser, and all the other things she said about me."

His gut tensed. He couldn't bear that she should think of herself in those terms. "Don't say such things."

"I have to because they're true. If I'd spoken the truth from the very beginning, none of this would have happened."

It was killing him. He gritted his teeth and focused on the road ahead, following the motorbike driven by one of his men which would lead him to the airfield. He couldn't think about his pain now. His focus had to be her.

She must have mistaken his silence for disbelief. Because he felt her hand on his arm. "I'll make things right between us. I promise."

"Stop talking, please." He risked a glance at her face. It looked deathly. A trickle of blood ran down the side. He cursed under his breath, angry that he'd taken her impulsively with him. He should have had someone accompany her, to make sure nothing happened to her.

"Only if you say it's okay. That you're not angry." She winced as if her head were thumping.

"It's okay," he murmured, feeling quite the opposite.

He put his foot down and the car skittered over the shifting sands.

"And I'm not angry with you." He swallowed. "I'm just terrified that I nearly lost you." He glanced at her before staring back at the road. "I can't allow that to happen again, Samantha. You must promise me never to stray again. Promise me."

But there was no answer and, when he glanced at her, she was leaning her head against the side of the car, her arms around herself, and her eyes closed. He could see from the tension in her arms that she hadn't fainted, and he also knew that now wasn't the time to press his demands. They would have to wait until later.

CHAPTER 12

*D*espite the matron of the exclusive hospital's best attempts to make Zeeshan leave Samantha alone, Zeeshan stayed by her side. Wild horses couldn't have dragged him away. His only concession was to allow a curtain to be slid between them while she was being examined. The matron was scandalized that they weren't married. She didn't understand that, in his mind, they were. No piece of paper could bring them any closer. She also didn't understand one of the driving forces for being by her side and keeping hold of her hand around the curtain as she was being checked out. Guilt.

Zeeshan knew he'd done everything wrong. He'd hunted her down when he'd discovered she was pregnant with his child and he'd brought her to the palace and practically held her captive. He'd persuaded himself it was because he couldn't bear to lose his child. But it was more than that. He could bear to lose *her*. And he'd used the child as an excuse to keep her.

He was trying to be *not* like his father but, in his actions, he'd been as bad as him.

And, if he married her, he'd be doing even *worse* than his father. Because he knew better, and yet still he wanted this more than anything. But he had no right, after all that had been done to her, to cage a beautiful bird like Samantha.

The decision had to be Samantha's. Once he could be sure she was safe from any external threat, he had to give her her freedom. Otherwise she'd grow to hate him. Otherwise the intensity of their passion could twist and become an intensity which resembled resentment and hatred. He knew this. He'd seen it in others. And he'd created a situation where it could happen to him.

He had to put things right or there would be no peace, no love, no future, for any of them.

As his mind raced on all of these things, deciding on what he should do for the best, he continued to hold her hand while she slept, and to stare at her beautiful face. Her high cheekbones, once tanned, were now bruised and hollowed beneath. It broke his heart. He felt he was responsible for seeing this beautiful bird, damaged and fallen from the sky. She no longer soared, high on top of a wave, skimming life with an irresistible energy. Instead, she lay inert, in a hospital bed, with the future of the life inside of her in balance.

By the time she awoke, and her face broke into a heart-breakingly gentle smile, he knew what he had to do.

IT TOOK three days in the hospital before the doctors agreed that she could leave. At first she'd felt relieved to be safe and cared for. She'd felt weak and fragile. She wasn't used to feeling fragile. It was only when the doctors had finished a series of tests on her baby and pronounced that it had suffered no after effects of Samantha's trauma, that she realized how much tension she'd been holding. But even that didn't surprise her.

What had surprised her, more than surprised, was that Zeeshan hadn't made an appearance. She'd been vaguely aware of him all that first night and the nurses had told her how attentive he'd been. How he'd refused to move. But then, after she'd woken up that first morning, he'd said he was sorry, but that he had to leave her. At first she thought he'd meant he had work to do. She could hardly argue with that. He was king and in Ahmar that wasn't a figurehead role. He was a working king—and he was a working king with a political situation to deal with.

But, as she gathered her things and was escorted to the waiting vehicle by Zeeshan's assistant, *not* Zeeshan, she knew something was definitely wrong. Something had changed. And she hadn't the first idea what.

As they drove through the palace gates and into the now familiar concourse, she felt as if she were coming home. At that moment the sun rose above the minarets and spires which spiked the skyline, and the dark indigo horizon of the sea. The air was bright, not like it had been in LA, and she could smell the sea. And in that moment she allowed herself to accept the knowledge she'd known all along—she belonged here, in this place, with this man, like she'd never belonged anywhere else. She sighed. It was a relief to accept that knowledge.

She got out of the car and looked around, frowning as she looked in front of her again and walked inside the palace. Something was definitely wrong. Why wasn't he here to meet her?

After his assistant had passed her bags to the maid to unpack, she plucked up courage to ask him.

"Could you tell me where the king is?" she asked, in a voice she hoped sounded more confident than she felt.

Was it her imagination or did the assistant briefly look uncomfortable?

"I'm afraid I cannot."

She stood taller, indignant. This man was one of the few who knew of their relationship. "Cannot or will not?"

No emotion showed on his face. He was the consummate politician. "Both, madam." He gave a cursory bow. "The maid will look after your needs. We are all very happy to see you so recovered from your ordeal."

She could see in his eyes that he meant it. He may be the king's man, but his best wishes for her were definitely genuine. But it still didn't make her happy. "Could you please tell the king that I wish to see him. Urgently," she added.

He bowed again. "Indeed, madam."

She grunted disconsolately and poured herself a coffee from the tray a maid had left on the table. She picked up some food and wandered outside to the terrace and sat down to think.

What the hell was going on? Was he still mad that she'd left the palace without permission? Yes, that had been stupid. Hindsight was a wonderful thing. Maybe he was still mad that she'd only got together with him on a dare. She closed her eyes with embarrassment. The old Samantha seemed like a different woman. She realized now that the turning point had been meeting Zeeshan. Ever since that moment she'd felt centered, like she had a point in the world which was her place—not just geographically, but emotionally.

She sighed and took another sip of the strong coffee. Zeeshan certainly had a lot of things to be angry with her about. But surely the connection they had could overcome that? Surely he wouldn't let these things come between them?

She'd make sure they didn't.

She jumped up and went to the bedroom where she could hear the maid sorting through her clothes. She frowned. "Why are you getting my traveling things out?"

The maid gave a quick, uncertain smile. "You've been summoned to His Majesty."

Samantha frowned, not understanding. "Summoned?" She grunted softly and shook her head, trying to understand. She turned away, not wanting her maid to see her confusion. She fixed her gaze on the horizon, which was now streaked with brilliant strands of color. "For what reason?" She kept her back to the woman.

"I know not, madam," said the woman. "All I know is that I have been instructed to pass on this message to you. The prime vizier has asked that you come immediately."

Samantha looked at the clothes the maid was holding out. They were thicker than normal, clothes for traveling. "I think a lighter abaya might be more appropriate in today's heat." She plucked something out of the wardrobe and held it up. "I thought this might be suitable." The maid looked positively frightened now, as if she might reject the suggestion.

"I've been instructed to select this." Again that flicker of unease across the maid's face.

Samantha brushed a hand along the fine wool of the robes the maid held out. Her mind raced as she tried to understand what was happening. "But these are for traveling." She handed them back to the maid. "I don't believe I'm going anywhere this morning."

"I'm sorry, madam. I'm simply following orders."

"And I am sorry that you don't feel able to confide in me what is going on. I thought we were friends."

Tears glazed the maid's eyes. "I don't know for sure, madam. All I know is—"

Samantha reached out and touched the woman's arm. "Tell me what it is you know."

The woman's shoulders drooped and her smile fell. She shook her head and Samantha took the clothes from her, dropped them on the bed and led her into the sitting room.

By the end of half-an-hour, Samantha's initial joy in the morning and high hopes for the future had been dashed. Instead, a sense of doom settled in her gut. She tried to piece together what was going on behind the scenes as her maid talked to her, but all she'd been able to glean was that there were plans afoot and they didn't include her staying here.

Samantha rose and picked up the traveling robes from the bed and tossed them in the direction of the wardrobe. "These won't do at all. I'm not going anywhere."

ZEESHAN PACED UP and down the room. He'd been awake all night trying to figure out what to do, and it always came back down to the one thing. He had to let her go.

Samantha had told him in no uncertain terms that she'd only ever wanted one thing from life—and that was her freedom. Freedom to do what she wanted, freedom to be who she wanted to be. After the strange upbringing given her by her parents, she balked at any kind of restriction, even if that restriction was a normal family life. Because, God knows, that was all Zeeshan wanted with her now.

No, he had to give her the freedom which she craved because, unless he did, he would be worse than his father. Unless he did, she'd grow to hate him. And he couldn't bear watching her expression turn from a loving one to that of a frightened animal, caught in a trap. Eventually the love would twist into hatred, and resentment would feed that hatred until their life would be a nightmare—exactly like he'd witnessed with his own mother, trapped by a man who she hated, a man she'd once loved.

No, there was only one way to do it. Sometimes lying was the most honorable way to deal with the situation. The end always justified the means.

His intercom buzzed and he glanced at it. She'd arrived.

He sat down at his desk, picked up a piece of paper and studied it. He didn't read a word—they all blended together. But she didn't need to know that. He slammed his hand on the intercom and grunted his assent.

He knew it was her before she entered the room. There was no one else who wore her perfume—natural and lemony. His mouth watered at her scent despite himself. But he forced himself not look up at her, not acknowledge the effect she had on him in any way.

He signed a piece of paper—despite the fact he had no idea whether he needed to sign it or not—and placed it with careful deliberation to one side. He then picked up another document and studied it, imagining what she was thinking.

He didn't have to imagine for long.

"I know what you're doing, Zeeshan," she said in a brisk, matter-of-fact voice. She stepped forward, her abaya causing a breeze to shift towards him, intensifying her scent. He had no choice but to look up. She stood above him now. And he realized it had been a mistake to remain seated. She had the upper hand.

But even that wasn't enough for her. It appeared she wanted to come even closer. She leaned forward, and gripped the edge of the desk. Slowly he rose so she had to look up to him.

"I know what you're doing," she repeated.

"Good," he answered. "That will save me the bother of asking you to leave."

She knew. He could see in her grim expression that she had anticipated what he'd was going to say to her.

"The only thing I don't know is why you are doing it."

"Ah, I thought that was obvious," he said. "Because I no longer wish you to be here."

For the first time since she'd entered the room, her fierce

expression cracked a little, revealing a pain she could no longer disguise.

"I understand that. But why do you no longer wish me to be here? When I was away you couldn't wait to bring me back."

"You had been kidnapped. It was my duty."

She stepped back, folded her arms and rested her weight on one hip. She shook her head. "Your duty? And so, what are you telling me? That it is your duty now to send me away again? Because I know you don't want me to go. I know you love me. You may fool your mind, but you can't fool your body. When you come to me at night I know what it is telling me." She leaned in to him again, and he wished she hadn't. "And it is definitely not telling me to leave."

It took all of his resolve not to weaken. But he knew that, in the long run, it would not be right. He shrugged, pulled an envelope toward him and then pushed it across the table toward her. "You can believe whatever you like. But I wish you gone and there is enough money in the envelope and investment information to make you and our child comfortable. The air ticket is for Dubai. You won't be far away. I will still see my son. But I will not see you."

"I don't believe you. Family is everything. You'd really allow me to walk away with our son?"

"I am not just allowing you, I am telling you to go. It is for the best."

"Best for you, or best from me, or best for our son?"

"For everyone concerned."

For one long moment he held her gaze. As he watched emotions flit across her eyes and face, he literally watched her resolve dissolve. But why was he so surprised? That was what happened when a tender thing came into contact with an unyielding object. At some point it had to realize that the two did not go together. That the unyielding object blunted and trapped the tender thing. He recognized it, so why didn't she?

He broke the gaze by reaching out and flicking a switch on the intercom. "Miss Cross is about to leave. Please show her out."

The door immediately opened and two of his guards entered the room and came and stood either side of her. She shook her head

"Really, is this what it's come to?"

For the first time since she'd entered the room, his firm resolve cracked under the laser-heated emotional glare of her eyes.

And then she looked down at the photos ranged around his desk and pointed to one.

"Do you think she would approve of all of this?"

"It's because of her I'm doing it." He stepped away, suddenly realizing he'd been trapped into speaking the truth. He beckoned to the guards. "Escort Miss Cross to the airport. The jet is waiting for her."

His phone rang loudly, piercing the tension, and he answered it, glad of a diversion. Unfortunately it was Adam. He turned his back to Samantha, but he could feel her gaze lingering on him before she turned, dismissed the guards with a flick of the hand, and left the room.

Good. He'd done what he'd set out to do. There could be no other outcome. He, of all people, knew better than to expect someone like Samantha to be happy in a place like this, with a man like him.

Now all he had to do was tell Adam that he'd sent her away.

. . .

SAMANTHA GLARED at the guards and, ignoring them, swept through the passageways, heading for the gardens. She had a feeling that her bags had already been packed, that she was the last piece of the puzzle to be fitted. Well, they'd all have to wait. Because she was in no mood for being conciliatory. She began pacing back and forward across the garden, winding up her annoyance with Zeeshan. She knew he didn't want her to go. There was nothing in this world he could say which would make her believe him. He was doing this for one reason only—because he thought it was best for her. She knew him. Better, apparently, than he knew himself.

She was startled by a sudden sound. Hoping it was Zeeshan, come to his senses, she turned around sharply. But the door was closing behind Adam, who came over to her. He shook his head.

"My brother is mad, but I'm guessing you know this already."

She exhaled loudly, showing her exasperation. She held her hands up in the air, in an expression of helplessness. "He's told me I have to go, that he doesn't want me around anymore."

"Well, that's nonsense. You must know that."

"I think I do. But he doesn't seem inclined to change his mind."

"That's why I'm here."

She cocked her head to one side in query.

"To explain things which Zeeshan, no doubt, has neglected to tell you. Things which have made him the man he is today. Stubborn, principled and prepared to do anything that's right, even if it means it will hurt him."

Samantha indicated the seat. "Please, sit down. I would love to hear what you have to say." She sat down, and watched as he followed suit. "Although I have to say I think I've probably guessed the things he hasn't told me."

He gave her a quick, acute glance. "I'm sure. But I don't want you to be in any doubt as to why he's acting this way."

He hesitated and she took pity on him. "Tell me about your father."

He sighed. "You're right. It all stems from him." He sat forward, resting his arms on his legs in a casual fashion which belied the intensity of his gaze, which skewered her. She pitied the woman Adam loved. She knew, whoever it was, she wouldn't stand a chance against that gaze, which fronted a will which was indomitable. But all she felt for him was concern and intrigue. His knowledge was the key to understanding the man she loved.

"Go on," she said gently. "Please, tell me whatever you can to help me understand."

He nodded and looked up above her, as if going to a different place in his head. "Our father was raised strictly by a tutor, spending much time alone in the desert with him. Our grandfather always regretted it. Apparently the tutor died under mysterious circumstances, but not before the damage was done." He shrugged. "Or maybe he was just born a bastard. Whatever." He looked at her directly again. "My father ruined the life of just about everyone he came into contact with."

"Including his family."

"*Especially* his family. He needed to control everyone, needed to make everyone bow to his will." He pressed his lips together. "Except one person. One person who he loved above everyone."

Samantha furrowed her brow. "Zeeshan?"

"Yes, Zeeshan. Zeeshan was his whole life."

"And how did Zeeshan feel about that?"

"To begin with, he trusted him implicitly. And, later, when that trust was broken and he understood the reality of his father's and mother's lives and personalities, he played a game, a game which proved extremely hard for someone as principled as Zeeshan."

"What kind of game?"

"He continued his relationship with his father, because he knew it was key to helping everyone else—his mother, his brothers, his sister, all the illegitimate bastards who our father had scattered around the country. And he did help. Rayan suffered most and Zeeshan did everything he could to help him and, for the most part, he succeeded."

"And you?"

He shrugged. "I got off lightly. But, sometimes, I think it was Zeeshan who came off worse than anyone. But, whatever, what he did worked... up till now. He cared for us all, and we thrived. And I've watched him keep everything in, until I saw a change in him six months ago."

She opened her mouth and sucked in the warm, fragrant air. "When he met me."

"Yes, when he met you. That was when something fundamental in him changed. Both Rayan and I saw it. I suspect Zeeshan was the only one who didn't. He met you, he cared for you, and he wanted to control you and keep you safe. Except it didn't work this time."

She shivered and warmed her arms with her hands. "I need to feel free. My upbringing wasn't exactly story book either. Well, not the *good* kind of storybook, anyway," she said, with a rueful smile which quickly vanished from her lips.

He reached over and touched her arm. "He's trying to change, he really is. That's what this is all about. Sending you away because he believes you crave something he can't give you."

"Oh, but he can," she said softly. "Because he's not the

only one who's changed. You see, I grew up with a terror of being trapped in one place with my mother. After my father died, I had to suppress everything to keep my mother on an even keel. It didn't work, of course. But now, everything's changed. I no longer see freedom as an expanse of nothingness, with no boundaries."

"What do you see it as?"

She closed her eyes to see better. "I see it as being with the people, and in the place, I love more than anything in the world."

When she opened her eyes he was smiling at her. "I hope that includes Zeeshan, because I've never seen him like this before."

"Like what?"

"In love. He's changed. You've changed him and that only comes from one thing—love."

"You sound as if you know a lot about the subject."

He quickly drew back his hand and jumped up, shaking his head firmly. "Me? I know nothing about the subject. Well, only in as far as my brothers are concerned." He looked around now. Suddenly it was his turn to look uncomfortable. "I have to go." He glanced back at her. "What are you going to do?"

She rose, and without thinking placed her hands on her stomach. "Stay here, of course."

"Good. I'll leave you to it then."

"Adam!"

He turned to face her.

"Will you tell him?"

"I think I'll leave that up to you. My wisdom only extends so far."

She watched him go, thinking that Zeeshan's youngest brother was far wiser than he knew, even if he didn't want to be. Adam had his own life to lead and his own battles to fight

—whatever they were—but at least he'd put her on the right path.

She walked quickly away from the harem. She had work to do while she waited for Zeeshan to come. Because, she knew for sure, come he would, and she wanted to be ready for him.

CHAPTER 13

Several hours later, Zeeshan had calmed down sufficiently to allow himself to be interrupted.

"What do you mean, she's still here?" asked Zeeshan, glaring first at one person then the other. "I told you to escort her to the plane."

The men shifted uncomfortably, looking from one to the other.

Zeeshan came around his desk, hands on hips, and glared at them.

"What's happened?"

The younger official cleared his throat, and tried to loosen his robe from around his neck. "It's Miss Cross, Your Majesty. She, er, declined your invitation."

A flare of annoyance at having his wishes thwarted shot through him. He wasn't used to this. "I wasn't aware I'd invited Miss Cross to do anything. What I *did* was instruct you to take her to the airport!" His voice rose with each word but he didn't appear to have the power to stop it. He looked at the hapless individuals and knew that they were even more incapable of making Samantha do something she didn't want to do, than he was. He muttered a vehement curse under his breath and turned away, pushing his fingers through his hair. What the hell was he going to do with her?

"Go to her and..." He trailed off. What could he get them to say that hadn't already been said? "No, I'll go." He began to walk in the direction of her rooms, when there were more uncomfortable coughs. He turned. "What is it now?"

"She's no longer in her rooms, no longer in the harem, Your Majesty."

"Then tell me where she is," he said, without turning around. He felt as if everything was slipping away from him. As if his world, which had always been so sure, so certain, was shifting beneath him. He couldn't turn to look at his assistants without revealing how utterly helpless he felt when it came to Samantha.

"She's had her things removed from her rooms."

"And?"

"They've been taken to *your* suite."

He closed his eyes as if he'd been dealt a blow and sighed. He'd wondered what she was up to, now it appeared certain. She was digging in. She had no intention of doing as he'd instructed. He didn't respond any further, merely changed direction and strode towards his own private suite of rooms. Or, at least, they *had* been private, until now.

SAMANTHA SAT BACK in the floral, upholstered chair and pressed 'send' on her email with a flourish. Okay, she had probably missed a huge chunk of the wedding preparations off her list simply because she didn't know what was required. But that could come later. What she needed to show was her intent. No, not just her intent, what *was* going to happen. There would be no way Zeeshan could cancel some of the things she'd set in train, not without losing face, not without admitting to the whole world that, although he loved her, he would not marry her. She couldn't see him baring his most private self in public.

There was a flicker of unease in her heart as she looked through her notes. But it was nothing compared to the sheer, desperate unhappiness she'd felt at the thought of leaving him. She wasn't going to leave without a fight and that fight would take place in the heart.

It had been a good few hours since Adam had left and she hadn't wasted a second of it. She wanted all the wedding arrangements to be initiated before Zeeshan knew anything about it. She'd immediately returned to the royal quarters and set herself up in what was once Zeeshan's mother's sitting room. It was a beautiful space, light and airy, decorated simply and yet feminine, and within view and sound of the sea.

She flicked through the notes on her iPad and grinned.

Flowers, tick.

Imman, tick.

Clothes, tick.

Guests, tick.

Feast, tick.

Samantha shifted the iPad to one side of Zeeshan's mother's desk and lightly fingered the pretty arrangement of feminine photographs. Most of them included Zeeshan at various stages of growing up. She picked up one and looked more closely at it, and smiled. He must have been around eight years of age when the photo had been taken. His mother stood beside him looking solemn, but his father, whose image she recognized from the paintings and photographs hanging around the palace, looked stern and yet very proud, his right hand firmly on Zeeshan's shoulder.

Zeeshan was smiling confidently at the camera, looking proud of the bird whose talons gripped his glove, while his other hand rested on his mother's arm. It would have been a sweet family portrait, capturing the moment when Zeeshan was holding his bird which had something in its mouth. He'd obviously been hunting and had succeeded, much to his father's obvious delight.

But his mother? Her head was tilted down and she looked up with wary eyes. Samantha's smile faded as she remembered that Zeeshan's mother had been having a dangerous affair for years and had suffered at the hands of her husband, the king. And that was without him knowing of the affair. She must have loved Zeeshan's birth father to have risked so much.

Samantha replaced the photo and picked up another in which Zeeshan was in his early teens. Gone was the smile and a hardness now shadowed his eyes. He'd grown tall, taller than his father even, and still had the look of pride and confidence, but it was tempered now with an experience which he shouldn't have had at that age. And Samantha instinctively knew that the photo had been taken after he'd discovered his mother with her lover.

His trust in the two most important people in the world had been destroyed. And it had made him the man she'd fallen in love with—damaged and hurting. But she knew all about those things and she fully intended to help Zeeshan heal.

There was a knock at the door and she looked up. She didn't think it would be Zeeshan because she doubted he'd know what she'd done yet. He'd be hard at work still and, she imagined, his staff would be reluctant to tell him that they'd failed in his instructions.

"Come in!" Her maid entered, escorting a couple of people she'd contacted about the wedding arrangements. She rose and shook their hands. "Ah, thank you for coming at such short notice."

The maid made a quick exit to carry out some of the other errands Samantha had given her, while Samantha discussed the food with this couple, who she needed to put at ease.

"Now, I want to organise a wedding banquet."

"Who is it for, if we may ask?"

She licked her lips. "It's for me... and the King of Ahmar."

She smiled at their reaction as they fumbled with their devices, bringing up the information she needed.

Samantha was beginning to enjoy this.

ZEESHAN HESITATED as he strode into his suite of rooms. He looked around, but couldn't find Samantha. Then he heard voices. He followed them until he stood outside the sitting room which had once been his mother's retreat from the world. Surely she wouldn't have dared?

He burst open the door to find that she *had,* indeed, dared and, not only that, she was in the middle of some kind of meeting, looking for all the world as if she belonged there.

"What the hell is going on?"

The two visitors jumped up, while Samantha turned to him with a smile. "Darling! I was just finishing up here." She turned to the others. "Thank you for coming. I'd be grateful if you could action the arrangements as per our discussion and let me know tomorrow how they're progressing. Thank you."

It looked like the two people couldn't leave fast enough. Samantha shot him a quick smile, rose and brushed down her abaya.

"There," she said obscurely.

Zeeshan frown deepened. "There what?"

She inclined her head and pursed her lips as if trying to figure out a reply. "There," she said slowly, "you go. As in…" She sighed and looked him directly in the eyes for the first time. "As in… it's time."

"Time for you to leave. That's what it's time for." He put his hands on his hips, trying to figure out what the hell was going on. There was a part of him which was relieved that she hadn't gone—bone-deep relieved—but he suppressed that part. That was the selfish part and he needed to think about Samantha now. He ground his teeth. "Samantha!" he said, in a warning tone.

She raised an eyebrow as if he were flirting with her. "Zeeshan," she said, stepping forward so he was forced to contend with not only her visual beauty, but also her fragrance and the depths of her eyes in which he was reflected back to himself. He filled her vision, and she filled his.

"I *thought* you'd be gone." He could hear some of the fight had left his voice. He cleared his throat. "In fact, I gave specific instructions for you to be gone."

She smiled, her eyes twinkled, and she gave a short laugh before shaking her head. The smile on her lips was relaxed as if she was in on a joke that he had no idea about.

"Well?" he asked, wanting her to say something, *anything*, which could explain to him what the hell was going on.

She stepped closer to him. A part of him wanted to step away, to not be anywhere near the temptation that was Samantha. Another, totally contradictory part of him wanted to grab her and make sure she never left him. He balled his hands into fists to stop himself from reaching out to her.

"Well?" she repeated, in that seductive voice of hers. "Maybe I decided I didn't agree with your specific instructions."

"I didn't ask whether you agreed or not."

"Darling, it may have skipped your notice but I am not your subject, I am an independent person who just so happens to be madly in love with you. I decided *not* to take you up on your offer of leaving."

He grunted with frustration, his fists tightening. "It was *not* an offer. And you may be in love with me at this moment, but that will change, I can assure you."

For the first time her brows tweaked together. "Is that what you're frightened of?"

How had she managed to turn this conversation around? He was accustomed to asking the questions and receiving answers. But Samantha had the aggravating habit of being able to turn the tables on him. He refused to play her game.

"Samantha!" he said in a warning tone. "I told you to go."

"And," she said, with a swing of abaya, "I decided not to follow your orders."

He glowered at her. He didn't like being reminded that he'd ordered her away. He was becoming more and more like his father. He might not be of his blood line, but it was obvious that the man had more of an influence on him than he'd either imagined, or wanted.

"I don't know what you think you can gain by going against my wishes."

"Gain?" She folded her arms and stood uncomfortably close. "Oh, that's easy." She reached over and brushed an imaginary speck from his clothes. He took a quick intake of breath. How could a simple, light touch from her fingers create such havoc inside him? He could easily imagine that shimmers of light extended from her fingers, an extension of her soul, sending shards of electricity through his system.

"Nothing is easy," he ground out.

Her smile slipped to sympathy. He didn't like that. "Yes, darling, it can be. That's why I stayed." She placed her hands on her stomach. "Because we—that's me and our baby—both belong here, with you. It's that easy, it's that simple."

"I *won't* keep you captive here."

"Indeed. And I wouldn't allow you to. But I freely choose to be with you. You, this place, this country, is my home now. Nowhere else." She placed her hands on his shoulders, before snaking them around his neck, pulling him, not so very gently, toward her. "Zeeshan, will you marry me?"

He didn't think he'd heard correctly at first, and simply stared at her. She smiled. "It's customary to answer such a question."

"You can't ask me to marry you."

Her smile broadened. "Why? Because you're king, always in control, always so self-disciplined and so lacking in spontaneity?"

He frowned. She was correct on all counts, but hell would freeze over before he admitted it.

"Darling Zeeshan. I love you and you love me, and we are expecting our baby. Plus"—she pouted a little, it was all that was required to melt the last of his resistance—"I've set in train the wedding arrangements."

His eyebrows shot up, but before he could respond, she rolled onto tiptoes and pressed her lips to his, holding him in position with her hands around his neck. He immediately relaxed his fists, placed them around her back and deepened the kiss. All thoughts fled except how right it felt. Eventually they moved apart.

"So," she said. "What do you say?"

He touched her cheek wonderingly. "You would really marry me? After all the wrong things I have done, and continue to do? I'm controlling—"

"Sometimes that's fun," she said with a grin.

"If I love someone I tend to hold them too tight, keep them too safe. If you feel trapped you will leave."

"I don't feel trapped. But I would like to know one thing, too."

He pushed her hair aside to better see her. "Which is?"

"I need to know if you trust me?"

He nodded. Of course he did. He'd trusted her with his heart, and everything else from the first moment he'd seen her. Fate had tried to convince him otherwise, but it seemed, his heart had been right the first time. Despite what the Russians could have done to her, she'd refused to tell them his secret. "Yes, of course I do. I'd trust you with my life and the life of our baby."

"But do you trust me with your heart?"

It seemed kissing her was the best way to answer that.

"Then you'll marry me?"

"Of course. My heart is yours to do with whatever you wish. You wish to marry me, then we will marry, even if I do not deserve you."

She pulled a face. "I've hardly been an angel."

"I'm not interested in angelic," he said, pressing his hips to hers. She giggled and the giggle turned into a moan as he captured her mouth once more with his.

She pulled away, her face serious now. "That's good, because I'm feeling a little devilish right now." She took his hand and pulled him towards the bedroom.

It wasn't until much later, after they'd ignored phone calls, knocks on the door, the sun rising and falling until only dusk and a night full of promise lay ahead, that they lay in silence on the bed. Naked. Sated from lovemaking, she lay with her head resting in his arms, as he stroked her.

"Just promise me one thing, Zeeshan. There will be no more secrets between us. A thing with secrets is shrouded and unclear. I want everything to be clear between us."

"I promise. If I think it, I will tell you."

She propped her head up on her arm and looked at him

with definite mischief in her eye. It looked like the devil in her had popped up again. "What are you thinking now?"

A part of him hardened, betraying his thoughts. She glanced down and placed her hand over him. "I see. In that case..."

EPILOGUE

Samantha stroked her baby's soft downy hair, smiled and looked up at Zeeshan.

"He looks exactly like you!" She grinned at his brief frown. He stepped into the room from the shadows where he'd been watching her.

"How did you know I was here?"

She shook her head. "Zeeshan! Surely by now you realize that I am a witch and have extrasensory perception—but only where you're concerned," she added, with a wide grin.

"Of course. The woman who cast a spell on me." He returned her smile and kissed the baby's head. "If he looks like me then he must be extremely handsome."

Her eyes sparkled with mischief. "Either that, or you have a squashed up face with scanty hair."

He hooked his fingers around her neck and brought his head on a level with hers. "You, Samantha, are in a very strange mood. What is it you are trying to do?"

"Tease you, Zeeshan."

"Nobody teases a king."

"Except his wife. And that is one of the primary duties of a wife. To make sure her husband, the king, keeps humble."

He laughed and she did too, because one thing Sheikh Zeeshan ibn Mohammed Aziz, King of Ahmar, wasn't, and never would be, was humble.

"If you wanted a humble man you should have fallen in love with someone ordinary."

"Maybe it's not too late."

His eyes narrowed and he kissed her hard on the lips. "Now that, wife, is enough teasing for one day. Because you know I will not allow you to fall in love with anyone else but me."

She grunted and he liked the sound of it—low, murmuring, orgasmic. "You seem very sure."

"I am. Because as well as being a proud man, I am also very sure of myself, and sure of you, too. Especially when it comes to how to manage your body."

She arched an eyebrow and passed the now sleeping baby to the waiting maid, who was trying to stop herself giggling at the heated exchange between Samantha and the king.

She glanced at the maid as she closed the door. Then turned her entire attention back to Zeeshan. She didn't do up her dress, but kept her full breasts exposed. She hooked her hands behind her head, lay back and looked up at her man. "I'd quite like to see how you manage me."

He kissed each breast and lifted up her robe from her ankles, sweeping up her legs with his fingers until they found their target. "It won't be just seeing you'll be doing, but feeling, and maybe tasting, too."

It was her turn to lose her smile, and his turn to turn one on as she succumbed to his lips and his fingers and... other parts, which showed her that he could, indeed, manage her most successfully.

AFTERWORD

Dear Reader,

I hope you enjoyed Zeeshan's and Samantha's story. The secrets continue with the next book in the series:

The Sheikh's Marriage Trap

Feel the need for more sheikhs? If you haven't already, why not check out my **Desert Kings** or **Sheikhs of Havilah** series? They both feature sheikhs who are used to their every command being obeyed, falling in love with strong women with minds of their own. Sparks fly, and their 'happy ever afters' aren't easily achieved, especially when you add a dash of mystery and intrigue...

Desert Kings
Wanted: A Wife for the Sheikh
The Sheikh's Bargain Bride
The Sheikh's Lost Lover
Awakened by the Sheikh

Happy reading!

Diana

~

THE SHEIKH'S MARRIAGE TRAP

BOOK 3 OF SECRETS OF THE SHEIKHS— ADAM AND JASMINE

A sheikh dedicated to pleasure, a woman intent on revenge, a love that demands the impossible...

Sheikh Adam ibn Mohammed Aziz enjoys a life of wheeling and dealing, seducing and flirting. So what if his half-brothers claim it's Adam who most resembles the father they've all grown to hate? He's only doing what comes naturally, and loving women happens to come *very* naturally to him. So long as the women understand that they can never touch his heart. That's why an arranged marriage will suit him nicely. The only requirement of him by his prospective wife is that he be untainted by scandal. And he's been too discreet to allow any scandal to attach itself to him. So far, anyway.

Half-English, half-Ahmari, librarian Jasmine Delaney flirts with Adam for one reason only—he caused her beloved sister's death. Jasmine and her family will never be the same again and she needs the handsome Adam to understand the pain his careless affairs have caused. At first she's not sure how she can do this. But all becomes clear when she discovers his Achilles Heel—he must appear to be free from scandal. So she decides she'll give him a scandal which will destroy his future. Perhaps then he'll understand, in a small way, the grief his womanizing has caused.

But the best-laid plans of a vengeful woman can go astray, especially when she finds herself in a setting of exquisite beauty, in the company of a consummate seducer who has spent his life perfecting his ability to give and receive pleasure...

Buy Now!

Secrets of the Sheikhs

Italian Romance

The Italian's Perfect Lover

Seduced by the Italian

The Passionate Italian

An Accidental Christmas